NIGHT OF THE COMET

THE OFFICIAL NOVELIZATION

CHRISTIAN FRANCIS

based on the screenplay by **THOM EBERHARDT**

echohorror.com

CONTENTS

FOREWORD

BY THOM EBERHARDT

I'm the guy who wrote and directed *Night of the Comet* ("*Comet*," to save space here). I'm also the guy who continues to be surprised by that little movie. The latest surprise is this novelization of the screenplay, 40+ years after the movie was in theaters.

After leaving ten years of Public Television behind, I wrote and directed my first screenplay. While the movie made it into release, it was gonged by every critic with comp tickets and a typewriter. It was in and out of drive-ins in a nanosecond, and rightfully so.

The script was slow, moody, and grim. Too late, I realized I don't do "slow, moody, and grim" very well.

Second chances are rare. I knew I wouldn't get hired just because I wanted a second time around. I needed another script under my arm as bait—this time, one I liked. As a normal, mid-century ten-year-old, I was lucky enough to be right in the middle of the golden age of low-budget monster/horror/outer space movies. A new one was in theaters weekly, and so were me and my buds, mostly to catcall the monsters. However, a subset of these movies could be unsettling, even scary.

The "Empty City Movies" were set against the backdrop of an intact, undamaged, big city whose entire population inexplicably vanished overnight. One in particular stayed with me well into adulthood: *Target Earth* (1954). It was painfully low-budget, but the first ten minutes were riveting. A frightened woman wanders through a silent city (L.A.), calling for help and getting no answer. Creepy indeed. Unfortunately, the film sank like a rock when a giant plywood robot showed up, and the U.S. Army (three guys in a jeep) rode to the rescue.

Ok, an empty city movie, but how to avoid slow, grim, and moody? The answer as I saw it: Pacing, Attitude, and Audacity.

Attitude and audacity were handled by swapping out a single, frightened woman for two Valley Girl sisters, Regina (17) and Samantha (15), who could handle automatic weapons and were more or less proficient in Kung Fu.

A big surprise: Thomas Coleman, a partner in Atlantic Realizing Corp., wanted to make what was then titled *Teenage Comet Zombies (B movie homage)*. I didn't know Tom, Atlantic, or how they got the script. It turned out that, wanting to help, my assistant handed the script to a friend, who handed it to another friend, and so on. Amazingly, the script ended up exactly where it needed to be.

Atlantic Releasing had a recent hit with the low-budget movie *Valley Girl*. They needed another *Valley*

Girl, only different, and they needed it fast. They got it, and I got the two writer/producers of *Valley Girl*, Wayne Crawford and Andy Lane. They weren't happy, to say the least.

Valley Girl launched Nick Cage into the bigs, ditto director Martha Coolidge. Wayne & Andy expected (and deserved) the same. Instead, they were handed *Teenage Comet Zombies*.

They didn't like the script, and they didn't like me. I'm pretty likable, so they probably read the reviews of my first movie.

They were sure there would be a big change after the first week of production when Tom Coleman would surely realize his "big mistake." Yes, there was a big change.

Atlantic tested the title *Teenage Comet Zombies*. Out of those three words, the only one the focus group liked was "Comet." "Night" always works in a title, so *Night of the Comet* was the new moniker. Also, Atlantic was happy with the first week's work.

Though my two producers would never let on, they did warm up to the movie and, by extension, me. Wayne & Andy went from looking over my shoulder to having my back (most of the time).

They were responsible for casting Catherine Mary Stewart and Kelli Maroney in the lead roles. These two young actresses understood their characters from the start, owned the characters, and still do. It's impossible to imagine anyone else as Reg and Sam.

When the company hired to handle promotion came on board, one of their executives called me. It seemed everyone in her office loved the picture. They totally got it. Then, after a pause and a sigh: "But nobody else will, Thom." OH, CRAP! The "Don't blame us" call!

They reckoned that no guy would take his date to see a movie about a couple of self-reliant sisters who could take care of themselves. There was no "Muscular Hero." I mentioned Robert Beltran, who played Hector, a Latino truck driver. He saved them at the climax. She replied, with the confidence of someone who'd gone to college, " No, he helped save them." I was in no position to argue. I dropped out of college right after flunking creative writing. I wanted to say, "Listen, lady, you got a bigger issue to deal with." I kept my mouth shut.

Night of the Comet is a "Mixed Genre" story, a whatzit. Most people who read the script liked it, loved it, or simply connected with it. The problem comes with selling it to a prospective audience. This is why Mixed Genre is considered poison. Was *Comet* an action movie, adventure, comedy, sci-fi, or zombie movie? I knew, but wouldn't say it out loud - *An urban fantasy adventure.* That wouldn't get anybody through the door.

A week before opening, TV ads started. Ad time was bought in *Twilight Zone* reruns and, of all things, *The Love Boat* reruns. A fast-paced montage was used as a visual for both. The clever trick was this: Ads in the Twilight Zone carried a heavy, threatening voice-over, *"Night of the Comet, 'dare to see it."* Love Boat carried the same montage but with a lighter, fun voice-over. Something like, *"Night of the Comet, come out and play."*

I have an original Comet poster in my office. Under

"NIGHT OF THE COMET" is a rendering of Regina looking out a mysterious open door. Under that—*"It was the last thing on earth they ever expected."*

Night of the Comet opened on 1000 screens nationwide, Thanksgiving weekend of 1984. It was a "muscular" release for a company like Atlantic. The L.A. Times review was practically a Valentine, as were most reviews. Over at PBS, Siskel and Ebert gave it two thumbs up. The budget for this little movie could have crawled under a duck. It was well under a million bucks. Opening weekend, it grossed 3.5 million. In the next four weeks, 14.5 million was added to the total. *Comet* was among the first movies to have a regular video cassette sales/rental release. It stayed in the top 50 cassettes for half a 5 year. It's certainly not the first low-budget show to do those kind of numbers, but *Comet* was "different." In the movie business, "different" is dangerous, but Tom Coleman wanted "different" and got it.

I started this by mentioning surprises. Here's one: The ads and poster for Crawford/ Lane's next movie contained: "From the producers of *Night of the Comet.*"

'*Comet* folded into 80's L.A. culture. A few years back, it was selected to screen for the opening night at the Los Angeles Film Festival.

After its first run in theaters, *Comet* started playing in small "art house" type theaters around L.A. For years, it's popped up in TV dialogue. "Dude, what do you think this is? *Night of the Comet?*"

Regina and Samantha were on "Garbage Pale Kids"

trading cards, and some lady started reproducing their costumes and weaponry for Barbie.

You might want to Google "*Night of the Comet* artwork," You'll find tons, done independently, a lot of it really good. Much of it is for sale on eBay, as well as t-shirts.

Who's buying this stuff? The original audience is in their 50's-70s.

I'll close with words from our family's middle school babysitter. She was new to my wife and me back then. Christy was showing her around the house, and she spotted a *Night of the Comet* poster.

"I saw that!" She said. "It was really scary."

Christy mentioned it was also fun. The babysitter agreed but added:

"The scariest thing about it is that could really happen."

Read this novelization for what it is.
Don't have any preconceived ideas of what it you might think
it <u>should</u> be, because that's where the gems lie.
In the humor and in the humanity of Reg and Sam.
Appreciate the uniqueness.
Because it's not going to be what you expect.

Catherine Mary Stewart & Kelli Maroney

"ALRIGHT, sports fans, it's time to lose your minds!" the voice of Mighty Mike blared over the radio in the manager's office of the El Rey Theatre. "The comet is on its way! And—get this—the light show starts at 2 a.m. sharp."

Melchor "Mel" Pazinki sighed and rubbed his eyes. At fifty-two, he never imagined he'd be managing a movie theater. He always figured he'd be running something bigger. A club, maybe. Something sleazy but profitable. Instead, he was here, skimming extra cash from a business that smelled like stale popcorn and cheap beer.

He didn't hate movies, exactly, but he sure as hell didn't care about them. To him, films were just another product, no different from overpriced popcorn or watered-down soda. The real money wasn't on the screen but in the suckers who paid to sit in front of it. And that night was no exception. The comet was just another excuse to cash in.

Normally, the El Rey was locked up by 11 p.m. sharp, but not that night. He had played this smart. He'd promoted a *Midnight Comet Screening* for one night only, starting at 11:15 p.m., wrapping just in time for customers to rush outside and catch the big event. They'd already paid for their tickets, their snacks, and if they wanted a souvenir, well . . . Mel had a stash of cheap comet-themed T-shirts ready to sell out of a box.

With his break coming to an end, he grabbed the pack of cigarettes from his desk, slid one between his lips, and lit up. He took a long drag as he buttoned up his jacket. His eyes moved toward the television across the room, its muted screen casting a pale blue glow into the room. A local news broadcast displayed a simple digital forecast of the comet's trajectory. A wireframe of Earth spun in its orbit while a thick red line arced dangerously close to it.

On the radio, Mighty Mike's voice kept rattling in its shrill tone. "That's right, folks. The Earth is about to go into full fireworks mode. We're talking the Fourth of July, New Year's Eve, and the Stones '81 concert all mashed into one. So, grab a drink, grab a date, and get outside because this ain't happening again for another fifty million years."

For weeks, the comet had dominated everything. Every paper and news channel hyped it up to fill otherwise slow news cycles. Every rooftop, park and parking lot had turned into a viewing party. Scientists and TV anchors tried to play it cool—and the fringe crowd?— oh, they were having a field day. According to them, this wasn't just a comet. It was a sign, a message, a warning.

Or Mel's personal favorite: a goddamn spaceship.

Late-night radio was buzzing with it. Talk show weirdos were ranting about how the government was hiding the truth, how the comet was really an alien craft using cosmic dust as camouflage. Some claimed transmissions had been picked up. Others swore they saw lights moving in the sky.

Mel? He didn't believe a single word of it.

But he knew a money-making opportunity when he saw one.

So, for the past few weeks, he had joined in with the madness. Plastered the lobby with oversized posters hyping the Midnight Comet Show. Offered a "special cosmic screening" of *It Came From Outer Space*, a 3D print he already had lying around from six months prior. The tagline practically wrote itself: *Prepare for Close Encounters of the Real Kind!* And at a premium price of $7 a ticket, it was a steal . . . for him, anyway.

The best part? He didn't even need to rent a new print. Just dusted off the old reels, slapped a premium price tag of $7 a ticket, and boom—full house.

And the real suckers were the guys who had already seen the movie before but were paying to see it again tonight—just because of the comet hype.

This was how you made money. Not by believing the crazy but by selling it to those who did.

He stubbed out his cigarette in the ashtray and took a last look at the television, where the comet's trajectory continued its slow crawl across the screen.

"Fifty million years," he muttered to himself. "Yeah, sure. Like I'll be around for the next one."

Outside, the film was already rolling.

And Mel? He was just waiting for the next sucker to walk through the door.

Inside the theater, the film was rolling to a full house. Teenagers, punks, and movie nerds filled the seats, all rocking their cheap plastic 3D glasses as the black-and-white film filled the screen. Some of them were locked onto the story, totally absorbed in its B-movie charm. Others were less interested in the screen as they flung popcorn, made out with their dates, or shouted at the actors in the film as if it were audience participation. It was a raucous, party-going night.

On screen, Richard Carlson delivered his line with gravitas. "I tell you, from its size and its appearance, this thing came from outer space!"

From the audience, a voice heckled, "That's what your mom said," setting off a wave of laughter around them.

With the film playing and the audience corralled into the theater, the lobby was a wasteland of waiting. Waiting for everything to end so the staff could clock off for the night.

Mel was standing behind a large stack of dollar bills as he counted the take on the concessions stand. He did not blink as he counted the success of the night. From his periphery, he could see a flashing light, but he did not need to look up to see what or who it was.

"Hey, Regina," he called out, mid-count. "Give that thing a rest, would ya?"

On the far side of the lobby stood *The Tempest*, a video game that shone a neon blue glow. Its hue flashed as *beeps* and *bloops* sounded around the player. The player in question was Reggie Belmont, her focus locked onto the flashing screen. She wore a fully buttoned usher's jacket, the uniformed look all the El Rey staff wore. A uniform she felt very uncomfortable in. But it did not stop her game. She stared at the screen intently, her feathered dark-brown hair framing her wide-eyed and determined gaze.

She shifted slightly with each movement as she twisted the controls with practiced precision. This was not her first or even hundredth go. This was *her* game. It didn't matter to her that she was at work. She was on the clock, but enthusiasm wasn't part of the job. With customers glued to the screen, she killed time like always.

"Regina!" Mel called out with an annoyed tone.

Reggie heard him. She just didn't care. She had long since stopped correcting him, knowing full well that him calling her Regina was just another way to try and annoy her. Not that she had any love for him either. She never called him by his name, at least not to his face. In her head, he was Melchorla. Like Dracula. But instead of saying *I want to suck your blood* in a thick Transylvanian accent, the version in her mind always sneered, "I want you to clean the popcorn machine."

Despite his call, she didn't move from being glued to the game as she continued to hammer the buttons. And he did not look up from the money. Both of their priorities were on full display.

"Are you listening?" Mel called out again.

"In a minute," she replied, still fully invested in *The Tempest*.

At the concessions stand, Mel quickly put away the money into a money bag and finally looked up at her. "You don't get paid here to do that," he moaned. "I want everything cleaned up so we can get out of here in time for the comet, okay?"

"Everything's *already* cleaned, boss," Reggie replied, not pausing her game for a second.

As if on cue, a loud electronic explosion sounded from the arcade machine. Reggie was zapped. The game was suddenly over, with a score of nearly one million. A phenomenal feat but not one good enough for her as she sneered and kicked the bottom of the machine.

"Dammit!" she seethed as the high score screen came up. She quickly hit the buttons to claim her latest score into third place. It already said REG was in that position. Her new score was taking that same place. "Replacing Regina Elizabeth Belmont in third place," she uttered softly, "is Regina Elizabeth Belmont."

She did not see the win in this, as, to her, she needed to beat the million-point mark.

Then she saw it . . . The one thing that made an anger well up in herself. An interloper. On the screen that always had REG at every score position was a new name nestled among the high scores. DMK.

"What the hell?" she muttered. "Who the fuck is DMK?"

Mel, meanwhile, had picked up a large black flashlight and put it on the glass counter. "Regina, if you've cleaned it all up, as you say, then take a flashlight and walk the house."

"Aw, Mel. C'mon!" she complained, turning to him. "They throw things at me in there."

"Tough luck," Mel said, shaking his head. "I don't want those weirdos cutting up the seats again."

Walking over to the counter, Reggie grabbed the flashlight, looking thoroughly unimpressed. She flicked it on and off a couple of times as if testing whether it was even worth the effort.

"You ever been hit with Dots, Mel?" she asked. "How about Milk Duds? You see, those things hurt. Or gum . . . You ever get gum in your hair?"

She let her gaze linger on his shiny, balding head for a moment, then smirked. "Oh, right. Guess you don't have that problem."

Mel grimaced. "Walk the damn house, Regina," he grumbled, waving her off away dismissively.

He turned, having about enough of her lip for one night. Still, he had to admit she had guts. More than most of the snot-nosed teenagers that came through here, clocking in, clocking out and barely even pretending to work. Reggie wasn't like that. She was a pain in the ass, sure, but she wasn't a pushover. And that? *That* was something he could respect. It was why he kept her around, even though she was a damn awful usher. Even though, half the time, she was more focused on arcade scores than customers, he still knew that if push came to shove, she wouldn't just roll over. And in a world full of suckers, that made her worth keeping around.

Up in the projection booth, the rattle of the 35mm projector filled the small dim space. The machine clattered with a rhythm as its sprocket drives spun, pulling the worn print through its mechanical cycle. The filmstrip flickered as it wound its way past the lens, casting images onto the theater's screen below.

Though the booth was cramped and stank of hot dust and nicotine, it had a certain charm—if you could ignore the dirt. Along one wall, stacks of film reels sat on shelves, each in metal cans labeled with a faded marker pen. Some were long forgotten, not screened in years, and some were still in rotation, just like that night's presentation.

The movie's soundtrack crackled through a speaker on the wall, tinny and distant, battling against the clatter from the projector. Somewhere within this noise, a voice cut through. A lazy, unbothered drawl belonging to one Larry Dupree.

Aged in his early twenties, he was a man who looked as if he was permanently stuck between stress and a nap. Wearing faded jeans, a half-unbuttoned shirt, and a white vest, he'd seen more late nights than early mornings. His hair was tousled, not quite messy but not exactly neat, like he ran a hand through it absentmindedly and never bothered to fix it.

Leaning against the bank of amplifiers that ran the sound into the theater, he held himself as if he owned the place, talking on the phone with an assured, confident tone.

"I'm talking about a mint condition print of *It Came From Outer Space*," he said. "In 3-fucking-D, man. You get me? You know as well as I do you got film freaks that would go down on you for a bootleg print of that. It's thirty fuckin' years old, and we're still showing it to a packed house."

He waited for a moment, listening to the caller on the other end.

"No way a hundred won't get it this time." He looked unimpressed. "Why? You think I'm gonna miss this comet thing waiting for you to bring it back for a crumby hundred dollars?"

At the other end of the booth, the door opened, and Reggie appeared with a smile, catching his eye.

"What's the plan?" she said in a hushed voice.

Cupping his hand over the phone, Larry returned the smile. "Here's the deal. When you leave, I'll let you back in the back door. Then, when I leave, you let me back in, and Mel thinks everybody's gone." He then removed his hand. "So, the film ends at 1:30. I'll have it back in reels and outside the back doors, in our usual place, by 1:50. And you have to have the print back by 6 a.m. at the latest. You got me?"

Reggie didn't look too convinced. "Spending the

night here means missing the comet," she moaned. "Not like there are windows in here."

Hearing her, Larry cupped the phone again. "Hey, it's not like you can't see it on the news tomorrow. It's just a blip in the sky. Who cares?" He then finished his call. "Okay, get your guy here in an hour."

Hanging up the phone, he smiled at Reggie. "What d'ya say? I'll give you fifteen bucks of the take?"

"I dunno," she shrugged. "If I spend the night here, then we'll wind up makin' it, just like we always do . . . And *then* you'll give me fifteen bucks. You know what that makes me look like?"

"An astute businesswoman?"

She looked back at him, unimpressed.

"The fifteen bucks is your cut of the job. Not for getting naked."

"*Fine!*" She rolled her eyes. "Just so we have that straight."

Larry walked over. "You'd be worth more than fifteen bucks, anyway."

He wrapped his arms around her and kissed her on the lips.

"How much am I worth?" she asked.

"Oh, at least twenty."

Across town, the living room of the Belmont household glowed with the flicker of a television screen.

The volume had been turned just high enough to drown out the sound of the party happening in the rest of the house and on the front lawn.

On the screen, a bland-looking presenter tried his best to come off like Carl Sagan yet was more like a bargain-basement knockoff version. If Sagan was a fine steak dinner, then this guy was a microwaved Salisbury steak . . . educational but with a strange aftertaste.

". . . After orbiting our sun for billions and billions of years, this marvel of frozen gas and metal now returns from the cosmos. Seemingly, its only purpose is to provide a night of spectacular entertainment for the population of Earth."

As she watched in a state of chronic boredom, Samantha Belmont slouched deeper into the couch, one leg curled under her, the other bouncing idly in time with the dull drone on the television. In this low light, the screen's glow flickered across her face, reflecting in her wide, restless eyes. Eyes that held all the impatience of a sixteen-year-old forced to endure another one of Doris's tedious parties.

Doris Belmont. Samantha and Reggie's stepmother. A woman who had taken over the house since their father, the colonel, had taken off to fight the bad fight. Shooting people who didn't deserve it for an unworthy country. That was, at least, how Samantha saw it. But both she and Reggie were trapped under the annoying grip of Doris.

Her stepmother's shrill laugh echoed from the kitchen, blending with the clinking of ice in cocktail glasses and the muffled thump of a record player churning out some adult-sanctioned music from decades ago.

Doris's party was, naturally, for the comet. Not that

she needed an occasion to open the colonel's house up to that horde of annoying elder yuppies she called her friends. And no amount of complaining from Samantha dissuaded Doris in the slightest.

"Now, Samantha, tonight was a big once-in-a-life-time event," her stepmother had said. "Besides, you're only sixteen. You don't get a vote on this."

Blah, blah, blah.

That's how that night's argument started. It ended with Samantha sitting in a sulk in front of the television as Doris did exactly what Doris wanted.

Each one of Doris' friends were on the front lawn, waiting in anticipation, huddling around their drinks, swapping scientific nonsense like they understood what the hell was going on. But all most of them really knew for sure was a big something or other was passing Earth. Anything more than that was regurgitated information they picked off people, like this Sagan-wannabe currently lecturing Samantha through the television.

She would have liked to have gone to a party with people her age but, instead, had been stuck inside, grounded, flipping channels on a television that barely got reception, landing on this dull broadcast with a host who looked like he'd been molded from plain oatmeal.

Instead of being dressed in party gear, she was wearing her usual tomboy-meets-Valley-girl-cheerleader mix. An oversized sweatshirt, a pair of cutoff shorts, with socks pulled up high. The same clothes she would wear on any evening.

Doris, meanwhile, was dressed in a brand-new brilliantly white Yves Saint Laurent pantsuit. Well, that's what she told everyone. The label said something different, *Yvonne St. Lawrence*. But she wore it as the real thing. It was a copy—a cheap copy, at that. Just like the man on the television.

Behind her, Samantha heard Doris walking out from the kitchen, flirting with Chuck, the slimy neighbor from across the street.

Standing there, dressed in a beige cargo jacket over a black T-shirt, Chuck thought he was a catch of a man, when, in fact, he was just a pudgy older man with a mane of fake dark hair and an equally large bank account. The latter was the most attractive thing Doris saw in him.

From outside, the excitement of her guests started to grow louder. Someone shouted about the comet getting closer, and for a brief second, Samantha considered joining Doris's crowd. But then she glanced back at the television.

Nope. If she was going to be stuck here, she might as well not subject herself to drunken assholes trying to grope her.

The telephone ringing on the sideboard quickly grabbed her attention. *At last. Something to do.*

Rolling off the back of the couch, she stomped over to answer the call.

"What?" she said into the receiver.

"Sam? You sound pissed," Reggie said into the pay phone of the El Rey.

She didn't have to ask, as she knew that her sister only sounded like that after a run-in with Doris.

"Doris and I had it out . . . again . . ."

Knew it, Reggie thought.

"What do you want?"

"Well, this is about Doris, and I need your help, Sammy."

"Oh, really now? My help?"

"Yeah, I need you to back me up. Can you tell her you know all about a field trip I have to go on with my . . . uh . . . science class or something, to watch the comet at . . . uh . . . the observatory, you know . . . Something like that?"

"She won't go for that bull."

"Sure, she will. She's probably toasted right now anyway. Last thing she'll wanna do is spend a second caring about what I'm doing."

Behind her, the lobby was being swept by another usher, the crowd of cinema-goers having left to find a spot outside. They could be heard from in here, whooping at the sky in excitement for the approaching light show. Mel had already taken his usher jacket off and was zipping up his coat, ready to shut up shop. Waiting for everyone to finish their jobs. He looked over, unimpressed by the fact that Reggie was still on the phone and not helping. He gave a slow, disapproving shake of his head—not that she noticed.

Samantha rolled her eyes and held the phone up in the air. "Hey, Doris," she proclaimed. "Telephone for ya!"

With a smile, Doris stopped flirting and motioned for Chuck to go outside, which he did like an obedient puppy. She then walked over, carrying her half-gulped glass of gin in one hand.

"Who is it?" she asked.

"Reggie," Samantha replied.

Doris's smile faded. "Jesus, she's not having car trouble, is she? I've drunk too much to go pick her up."

Samantha handed her the phone and replied flatly. "She's going to be out all night with her science class at the observatory or something. And I, apparently, know *all* about it."

Reggie rolled her eyes and let out a quiet breath as she listened to Samantha's painfully unconvincing attempt at selling her cover story.

"Yeah, hi, Doris," Reggie said.

"What's this crap about a science trip, Regina? I have seen no permission slips about this."

Oh great, Reggie thought. Not only was Doris going to make this difficult, but obviously, she was half-cut on booze and feeling invincible.

Reggie could tell instantly this was a losing battle, though she would fight valiantly nonetheless. "Well, you want me to do better in science, don't you?" she asked, trying to sound as innocent as possible.

"I want you home now. If you want to watch the comet, you can do it here from your bedroom window —and no supper."

Annnnnddd there it was. Doris's attempt at parenting. At 2 a.m. . .

Reggie should have stopped herself replying but just couldn't help it. "You know, Doris . . . it's not like you're my *real* mother. You know that don't you?"

With a forced, calm smile, Doris handed the phone back to Samantha and took a swig of her drink.

"Samantha," she then said coolly, "you and your sister share a lot of secrets, so share this one with her. If she's not home within twenty minutes, then I'm going to tell your father everything I know about her and this Larry Dupree character."

Slowly and not taking her eyes off her stepmother, Samantha spoke into the phone. "Did you get that?"

With a nod, she then hung up the receiver.

Doris's smile broadened victoriously. "Now, Samantha," she said coolly, swirling the last sip of gin in her glass. "Are you going to join the party or are you planning to sit here sulking like a brat all night?"

Samantha was exactly like her sister. She had trouble holding her tongue. So, just as anyone could predict, she spoke when she should have shut up. "Join your party? For what, exactly, Doris? So I can watch Chuck from across the street put his hands down your pants again?" She cocked her head to one side, eyes gleaming with challenge. "Talk about things Dad should know, not to mention his wife."

Doris's smile remained, unfazed at the threat. "Now, the fact that your father likes to fly all over the world playing soldier is not my fault. And besides, Chuck is nice to be around."

If given the power of hindsight, Samantha would have ended it here, then walked away with a polite smile and gone back to her business in front of the television. But that wasn't Sam. Not by a long shot. She would fight until it killed her. She instead smirked at her stepmother.

"You were born with an asshole, Doris," Samantha added, her smirk widening. "You don't need Chuck."

The words hung in the air for half a second. Just long enough for Samantha to see the shift in Doris's eyes, the flicker of something mean and unchecked.

Then the slap came.

A sharp *smack* echoed through the room as Doris's open palm connected with Samantha's cheek.

Slowly, she turned back to face her stepmother, eyes burning but smirk still intact. She lifted a hand and ran her fingers along her cheek, where the skin had already started to burn.

She didn't look away.

And then, just as Doris took yet another victorious sip of her gin, Samantha swung.

The slap she delivered back was harder, sharper, and caught Doris clean across the face. The glass slipped from her fingers and fell, gin splattering across the carpet.

Even the music from the record player suddenly seemed quieter. At least none of the guests were here to witness their fight. They were outside yattering, oblivious to any familial troubles.

Doris staggered back a step, stunned. She blinked, flexed her jaw, and then, without hesitation, her yuppie housewife façade cracked wide open. The girl from *Hell's Kitchen* came out.

With a sudden jab, Doris balled her fist, and punched Samantha square in the jaw.

The impact sent her sprawling back across the room, landing hard against the back of the couch.

Doris, meanwhile, shook out her hand, flexing her knuckles. "Peace through superior firepower," she grimaced before adjusting her pantsuit jacket, then smoothed her hair as she walked out.

Samantha slid down the back of the couch to the floor, rubbing her jaw and shaking her head at herself. "Damn," she mumbled, half horrified yet impressed at the punch. She *really* had to stop letting Doris bait her like this.

On the television, the budget Carl Sagan droned on. ". . . If this comet could only speak to us through the cosmos, what stories of wonder and beauty it would have to tell us. It could have seen alien civilizations rise and fall. Just think, the last time it crossed our path was when the dinosaurs disappeared."

Outside the house, twenty or so partygoers had gathered in the front yard and across the driveway. Their attention shifted between their drinks and the sky as they grew impatient to see the spectacle of the cosmos's free light show. A few picnic tables had been dragged out onto the lawn and were littered with half-empty paper cups, crumpled napkins, and the remains of cheaply catered finger food nobody had bothered to clean up the remains of.

On each person's head, a different glittery party hat sat askew. Some had alien bopper headbands, complete with glittery antennae swaying drunkenly with every movement; others wore the classic pointed cones.

They were mostly tipsy, some outright drunk, and their laughter filled the neighborhood. The air stank of booze, cheap perfume, and lingering cigar smoke. This was not the only gathering on the street, though, as all the neighbors who were not at other parties were out on their own lawns, waiting for the comet.

One of Doris's guests, a man in a loose-fitting Hawaiian shirt, the kind that suggested a very particular kind of midlife crisis, swayed slightly as he pointed to the sky. "Look! That was something, wasn't it?" he slurred. Though it wasn't clear if he had actually seen something or was just hoping to be the first to claim credit.

Next to him, another guest, clutching a plastic cup of questionable contents, squinted upward. "It's supposed to start any minute now," he answered confidently. "The news said about two-ten? Right?"

From the house, Doris emerged, slipping effortlessly through the small throng of her guests. She carried herself with the kind of boozy grace only achieved by someone who had many years of experience balancing cocktails and high heels. The altercation between her and her stepdaughter was heavily hidden through her touched-up makeup and happy demeanor.

She moved toward Chuck, who was nursing his whisky, looking skyward with mild interest. Turning, he smiled when he saw her. "It's starting," he said, sliding his meaty arm around Doris's waist. "Where were you?"

Doris swirled the remnants of her glass before downing the rest in one go. "The kids," she said with an annoyed shake of her head. "This is the last time I'll marry a guy with kids."

Chuck laughed, and Doris then laughed along with him, a little too hard, a little too loud. And then, almost absentmindedly, his hand drifted downward, slipping under the waistband of her pants. She barely reacted. If anything, she leaned into him. She didn't exactly care about the fact she was married or that Chuck's wife was at another party across town.

Above them, the sky quickly started to turn a very hazy shade of red. The darkness of the night lifted to reveal a surreal glow.

Then, suddenly, through the haze, a violent burst of light flared. The crowd gasped, eyes reflecting the display, their faces still in total awe.

BOOM.

A deep, guttural sound rolled through the streets, shaking plastic cups and rattling windows.

A moment of stunned silence.

Another flash.

Another explosive shockwave, like a giant hammer slamming against the sky.

These sonic booms. Things that the newspapers had foretold. They warned that the comet could release charged particles that would interact with Earth's atmosphere, causing pressure waves, which, in turn, would trigger the sound of thunder. Not that anyone here remembered that. They all looked taken aback as deep as the noise trembled through the streets. The earlier laughter and idle chatter had vanished, replaced with something unexpected: reverential silence and shock. Even the most cynical among them, the ones who had scoffed at the comet hysteria, stood, transfixed to what was above, humbled by the raw power of what they witnessed.

And yet . . . something felt wrong to each and every one of them.

Doris shifted uneasily, rubbing her arm. The skin beneath her fingertips wasn't just dry, but it felt . . . tight. Stretched too thin.

She gave a quick, irritated scratch and leaned into Chuck. "Boy, my skin itches," she said as she tried to shake it off. Chalking it up to a possible food allergy from the low-cost catering she put on. But the itch was quickly getting worse. The lights above flared again, bathing the yard in a blood-red glow as more booms started to fill the air.

Doris fidgeted, rubbing her arm furiously, pressing her nails against her skin, hoping she could scrape away whatever was beneath. Then a pulse of pain throbbed behind her eyes, sharp and sudden. She winced, then rubbed at them with her hands.

She was not the only one. This was happening to everyone here.

· · ·

The low drone of a radio crackled in the dark projection booth; its small speaker barely managed to contain Mighty Mike's endless chatter about the cosmic light show. His voice faded in and out, lost in the mess of rolling white static.

Tangled somewhere in the darkness, Reggie shifted slightly in the sleeping bag, her voice a murmur against the distant rumble of the crowds standing outside the El Rey, looking up at the sky.

"I don't like this, you know," she said in a whisper. "I'm always afraid someone will catch us."

Larry, lying beside her with a Cheshire cat grin, let out a lazy chuckle.

"See us how?" he replied, his tone thick with amusement. "There's no windows. No one can see through walls."

Reggie, though, wasn't convinced. She pulled the sleeping bag a little tighter around herself.

"Yeah, well, Superman could," she joked.

Larry turned toward her, then propped himself up on one elbow. "Not through these walls. They're steel. Used to be a fire law, you know . . ."

Reggie rolled her eyes. "Superman can and could."

"No, he can't. It's the one thing he *can't* see through."

She turned her head to look at him, eyes narrowing. "That's lead, numb nuts."

Larry grinned. "Whatever. Same shit. All solid metal."

Outside, a deep thunder rolled through the city,

faint but enough to be felt in here. The projector and reels of film shuddered ever so slightly.

Then, from the radio, Mighty Mike's voice cracked through the static, just barely audible—

"And to all the fine folks out in La La Land, I gotta tell ya . . . this is like nothing I've ever seen before . . . Wait . . . What is that?"

The signal was lost again in a wave of noise.

Larry reached over and gave the radio a light smack —not that it did anything to stop the interference.

Reggie rested her head back down. "Well, even if Superman can't see through here, I still don't like that we do it here, of all places. I'd like to be in a bed sometimes."

On the wall, hidden by the shadows, the clock read 2:25 a.m., and outside, unbeknownst to them, the city stood totally still and quiet.

CHAPTER
TWO

THE RED COLOR lingered in the sky as night bled into dawn. Los Angeles was used to unnatural skies, with the burnt-orange haze caused by the Santa Ana winds and the soupy yellowing gray of smog-soaked after-noons. But this? This was something else.

It clung to the city, buildings, and sidewalks. Not like fog or smoke. This had weight, a density that didn't drift or rise but stained everything it touched with an almost neon crimson hue. Everything had been colored by its presence.

By 6 a.m., the streets should have been alive with honking horns, drugged-up transients screaming at nothing, screeching tires, and the hurried steps of late workers. Instead, there was nothing—only an eerie, unnatural stillness.

Yesterday's newspaper, caught in the weak morning breeze, skittered across the asphalt street, tumbling end over end before coming to rest against a curb. Unread and unnoticed.

Despite the late-night revelry of the city, even then it was too still. Too quiet. Just emptiness.

In the Belmont household, up in Samantha's bedroom, the bed lay made. The curtains were still drawn, yet the eerie red glow of dawn bled through the thin fabric, casting a surreal light into the room.

On the nightstand, the clock radio's red digits glowed. 5:59 a.m.

The room was still, untouched by the usual stirrings of the morning. No muffled footsteps from the other rooms, no distant hum of running water from a shower.

Then, as the clock flicked to 6:00 a.m., a sudden burst of static rang out as the radio clicked on, shattering the peace with its garbled hiss.

". . . Some sort of trouble here . . . We'll have it fixed in a second. Just hold on to whatever horses you have," the voice of Mighty Mike announced. He crackled through the speaker, filled with white noise sounding very distant and fragmented.

And then a song played out through the crackles.

Upbeat, cheerful, and completely at odds with the feel of what was happening. The speakers warbled, the sound stretching in places as if the tape playing it was slowly warping.

"Okay, folks," Mighty Mike cut in over the song's intro. "Here to get you up and at them are the dulcet tones of Stallion with 'Let My Fingers Do the Talking.'"

. . .

Downstairs in the kitchen, also programmed on a timer, the coffeemaker switched on and gurgled as it began to percolate.

On the front lawn, the picnic tables remained exactly where they had been the night before, surrounded by the scattered debris of Doris's comet party. Crumpled napkins, half-empty cups, and discarded party hats littered the grass. The half-eaten food left on the paper plates would normally be a haven for the flies, but it sat untouched. The remnants of a celebration that had outlasted its guests.

The people were not the only things gone. There was no birdsong. No insects crawling through the grass. No neighborhood cats trying to pick through the food left out.

Then came the sudden hiss of water. A lawn sprinkler popped up from one of the well-manicured lawns and began its usual rhythmic spray, sending arcs of water across the dry grass. Another followed on a lawn farther down. Then another.

Across town, in a city park, the same thing happened as the watering systems whirred to life, misting the expansive stretches of lawns before the people were expected to arrive. Here, the swings and seesaws sat perfectly still, the chains untouched by even the wind. The slide was empty. The monkey bars, deserted.

The signs of Los Angeles moved as if the world had not changed. Storefront displays blinked on and off.

Neon signs flickered, selling drinks to no one. Traffic lights changed, stopping phantom cars, holding for invisible pedestrians. The city moved, even with no one left to see it.

But across all these locations, as well as the rest of Los Angeles, three things were unmistakably, undeniably wrong.

First, the sky. The sun's light, which would normally be golden and warm, was dust-cloaked and chilly. The new haze stifled the heat from warming up the day.

Second, the clothes. They were scattered everywhere. On the grass of the Belmont household. All over the park. On every street in every neighborhood. Clothing was strewn about where sky watchers stood at 2:20 a.m. A dress crumpled in the middle of the street. A pair of jeans folded at odd angles across a bus stop bench. A set of sneakers still tied, positioned neatly at a crosswalk as if someone had just been standing there.

The third thing was the unbelievable silence. It pressed down on Reggie like a weight.

Reggie stirred, half-conscious, still nestled in the warmth of the sleeping bag on the El Rey's projection room floor. The events of the night before were locked far outside the soundproofed walls of the theater. She had heard no booms from the sky, no cheers of the waiting crowd. Nothing.

The radio was still switched on and playing the

closing notes of "Let My Fingers Do the Talking" through the static crackles.

"Goddammit!" Larry moaned aloud as he came barging through the door from the corridor, switching the light on as he did, waking up Reggie with a start.

"What? What?" Reggie said, rubbing her eyes. "What is it?"

Larry was already dressed and had been up for a while. He was visibly annoyed.

"I've been standing out back for the last thirty damn minutes," he huffed. "That asshole hasn't brought the reels back yet. Bet that fucker is asleep . . . I'm gonna be in so much shit if they aren't back here by nine. Mel wants to rent it out to another theater."

Reggie collected her thoughts. She grabbed the pile of clothes next to her sleeping bag and got to her feet. Sluggishly, she began to dress, forcing her tiredness away. She was not used to functioning on less than three hours of sleep, but she was not going to get any more right then. Not with Larry being as angry as he was.

"Cut the guy some slack," she said, buttoning up her jeans. "Some people are late sometimes. Especially after last night."

But Larry was not hearing her. He was stuck in a paranoid moment. "If that guy's screwed up the film or something, we could all be in big trouble. We can't just replace it. It's 3D!"

Neither Larry nor Reggie noticed that, after the last song played, the radio had cut out.

Not to static.

Just . . . nothing. No sound. No broadcast. No Mighty Mike's usual chatter.

"I'm gonna jump on the bike and go over there," he said, resigning himself to the idea.

"Jeez, Dupree," Reggie said. "Don't I get an egg McMuffin or something first?"

"I'm sorry, but can you do me a favor?"

Reggie rolled her eyes. "I did you a big enough one last night."

Larry did not rise to her joke nor even acknowledge it. He was rooted firmly in his own worry. "We were lucky to get it out of here so soon after the screening last . . . I busted my ass getting that film back into the cans and off to him before the comet . . . If he calls while I'm gone, tell him I'm on my way over and I'm pissed! Okay?"

Reggie shrugged, given little choice.

Then Larry was gone, without another word.

She didn't like this kind of thing but had come to expect it with him. She had put off breaking things off with him for a while—not that they were official—and now, after this, she knew she would be better off alone.

At that moment, the radio sprang back to life again.

". . . Some sort of trouble here . . . We'll have it fixed in a second. Just hold on to whatever horses you have."

Reggie was not listening. Her mind went to her own troubles. Not her stepmother's threats. Not that Mel could choose to come back early and find her in the building, but her thoughts were squarely on *The Tempest*. The arcade game. *Her* arcade game. And that she had to get rid of the interloper on the scoreboard.

"Who the hell are you, DMK?" she mused quietly.

Larry mumbled to himself as he moved through the backstage corridor of the El Rey, his boots scuffing against the aged floorboards. The old theater always had a way of feeling eerie when it was empty, the absence of people making every creak and groan seem that much louder. But Larry was used to that. He was just transfixed on getting the film reels back.

"You trust people," he grumbled under his breath. "Then you get screwed over every time . . . every fucking time." Digging in his pocket, he approached the rear doors. He would just get on his bike ride across town. Get the reels and get back here before Mel was due to come in to open the cinema.

Just as he fished out his keys, a thud echoed from the other side of the door.

Larry paused.

Another thud. A dull, heavy sound.

His irritation turned into mild amusement. *Finally,* he thought. It was the guy bringing the film back. He must be kicking the door as his hands would be weighed down with the heavy reels. *About damn time.*

Larry rolled his eyes and stepped forward, leaning near the metal door. "That you?!" he called out. "Took you long enough. You were due here at six!"

No answer.

Just another thud hitting the door.

Larry grunted as he shook his head. *Rude,* he

thought. Unlocking the door, he reached for the handle and pushed it open.

"Alright, asshole, let's—"

He froze as his words suddenly failed him.

A thing stood staring back at him. A thing that did not look like a normal man. Presumably once a maintenance worker, from the look of his jumpsuit, work boots, and tool belt. But his skin was wrong.

He was too pale. Almost porcelain.

Once a Black man, his skin was like white-out, not pale as if he were sick. Not white like someone who had been drained of blood or had a condition like vitiligo. This was bone white. Chalk white. Bleached. Unnatural for any human. His lips were severely dry and cracked, and the hair that was left in uneven tufts on his head was also devoid of its pigment. But it was the man's eyes that held Larry to the spot.

They were blank.

No irises. Just pure, gleaming white, with only the faintest dark stain where the pupils should have been.

With barely time to react, Larry only managed to open his mouth, about to speak, as a claw hammer came down in a blur of motion.

CRACK.

Pain exploded through Larry's body before he could make a sound. His body spasmed as his legs kicked wildly outward. His balance gave way, and he tumbled outside. The keys in his hand clattered to the ground as he hit the concrete hard, half in the doorway, half sprawled over the outside step.

His vision blurred as his limbs jerked involuntarily.

Hands then grabbed his wrists.

Cold, deathly hands.

Larry was suddenly yanked outwards in a violent, dragging motion as his body convulsed weakly.

The heavy metal door to the El Rey had nothing to keep it open as Larry was pulled away and began to close under its own weight.

It clunked loudly as it locked itself again.

In the Lobby, Reggie had no idea what had just befallen Larry. She was too busy on her mission. Her mission was to score a million.

She hammered the buttons and yanked at the joystick as she played *The Tempest* once again.

"Okay, DMK, you're history," she said.

It took six quarters and a lot of expert timing, but finally—*finally*—she erased that smug little interloper from the high score ranks. Soon, every entry was back to saying REG. As it should be.

Her next move was obvious . . . celebration. And for Reggie, that meant a box of chocolate-covered malted milk balls. Any brand would do, and here, in the El Rey, they were her survival rations. She snagged a box from behind the concessions counter, popped a few into her mouth, and chewed as she wandered toward the front doors to look outside.

She hadn't noticed it before, being too preoccupied with her game, but something about the outside was different.

With the box of malt balls in one hand, she reached

out and cupped her other against the glass, peering out into the street.

There was no sign of anyone.

Reggie frowned and looked left.

Nothing.

She leaned farther as she turned right.

Still nothing.

Where the hell is everyone?

The city never slept, sure, but it also never just . . . emptied. Even at this hour, there should've been at least *some* movement. Some weirdo stumbling around. Some poor sap heading to an early shift. The occasional car, at the very least. But there was nothing.

Just that strange red tint on everything.

Her fingers found the door handle.

Could be a fire nearby, she thought. That was the last time she had seen a rusty-colored sky.

The door creaked as she pushed it outward and stepped onto the sidewalk. She left the door pushed wide, holding itself open. Tossing another malt ball into her mouth, she chewed slowly as she took a deep breath in, expecting to smell burning for whatever fire caused this. But there was no smell. She turned in a circle, looking around. No smoke either.

She knew not everyone would have stayed up for the comet—and, yeah, maybe some people were sleeping in, but this wasn't Christmas morning. That was still two weeks away. People had jobs to go to. People had places to be. Hell, the holiday's panicked shopping should have already started by now. People should have been fighting over whatever this year's must-have nightmare toy was.

She then noticed the coloring was on everything, not just the sky. Peering up, she squinted as she saw the thick blanket of crimson above her.

"Is that smog?" she asked herself as she popped another malt ball into her mouth.

The door behind her began to swing shut, creaking loudly, refusing to stay open on its own. It was another annoying quirk of the El Rey. Another thing in the building that didn't work.

Reggie heard the creak, turned, and leaped toward the door, hoping to grab it, but she was too late.

It clicked shut just as she grabbed hold of the handle.

With a grunt of annoyance, she jiggled the door, hoping that it would somehow magically open for her.

"Just great!" she moaned. "That's just real fucking fine."

Kicking the door to express her anger, she turned to look around. Evaluating her options.

The back door? she pondered before turning and purposefully walking around the building.

Down the filthy alley beside the El Rey, the walls were lined with large dumpsters. Here, the smell was as heavy as it always was. Day or night. Rain or shine. The stink from here was a constant, one that never shifted even when the dumpsters were emptied. It was just an ingrained stank in the very fabric of this alley. The sludge that congealed below the dumpsters seeped into the concrete and crawled up the brickwork. She usually joked that there was a monster out here who lived in the trash and that *that* was what the stink was, not the trash itself. That's the only reason it never left.

She held her breath as she passed by them, hurrying around the corner to where the back door was.

After rushing over to it, she grabbed the handle and hoped for the best.

Locked.

"Dammit!" she seethed as she kicked that door, too.

Reggie had probably kicked every part of the El Rey at some point. Doors, machines, people. If it annoyed her, it got a boot.

She didn't have much more time to get angry as she noticed something with her in the alley. Something that should not have been there. Larry's motorcycle.

Puzzled, she took a step closer, and as she did, her feet scraped against something metal. Peering down, she noticed Larry's keys on the ground.

Her brow furrowed as she stooped to pick them up. Larry never lost his keys. If anything, he was the type to check his pockets five times before even leaving a room. Maybe he dropped them in a rush, or maybe . . .

She glanced around the alley, suddenly uneasy. Had he been jumped? The city wasn't exactly safe, and this wasn't the best neighborhood to be alone at night. Hell, she'd seen guys get their asses kicked for way less than a motorcycle. But the bike was here.

Reggie's stomach sank. If someone had mugged him, where the hell was he? Did he run from something?

She straightened, suddenly feeling exposed by

standing out here alone. Her fingers tightened around the keys.

She needed to find Larry.

Then, just as she turned, she saw something else.

A dark, wet streak smeared across the pavement, trailing deeper into the alley.

Oil? Is that oil?

She peered at the dark liquid around her. Dark liquid she had only just realized she was also standing in. She could not see much about it, as the shadows here made everything indiscernible.

Stepping backward out of the wetness, she lifted her boot and wiped her fingers along the slick-covered soles.

Holding them up to the reddish light that peeked through from between the buildings above, she quickly realized that this was not oil.

It's *blood*?

And of course—with Reggie being Reggie—she did not run to find help. Instead, she looked down in shock at the pool on the ground and traced its path deeper into the alley. A way she followed. A way most people would run away from. *Is Larry hurt? Is this his blood? No . . . it can't be.*

Slowly, she walked, following the wet smear on the ground. It was so quiet here that the thump of her boots on the concrete reverberated around these narrow walls.

Noticing the dead end ahead as well as a collection of more stinking dumpsters, she slowed her steps to a halt.

Through the silence, another sound could be heard. Munching.

Slurping.

The sound of something eating very messily.

"Larry?" she called out quietly."

She squinted to see through the shadows around the edges of the dumpsters to her left, where the munching was coming from. She did not see much until something, *someone*, suddenly stood and came face-to-face with her.

The pale-eyed, ashen-skinned, cracked-lipped maintenance worker. In his hand, he gripped a large slab of bloody, raw meat. Meat littered with teeth marks. Blood from this chuck also dripped down from his mouth.

He watched Reggie with his blank eyes.

She had no idea what he was eating, but whatever it was, it dripped dark and wet from his fingers.

"Dude," she said. "That's gross!"

The pale man lowered his hand slowly and dropped the meat to the floor with a wet slap. He then started to smile. A weird smile. A smile that came on in small twitches.

His blank eyes fixed on her. His two milky white voids.

Is he blind? she thought. *Or is it something else?*

She'd seen drugged-up weirdos before, but this guy? This wasn't just some run-of-the-mill, late-night junkie.

What the hell's wrong with him?

She then realized that Larry, in all probability, did run from this guy. Dropping his keys and just abandoning her in the theater . . . *Figures.* And that blood? From that meat that the guy was chowing down on, maybe he raided a butcher's shop?

Feeling a sudden rush of trepidation, she stepped backward. "You're a couple of months late for trick or treating, pal," she nervously joked.

The man's horribly trembling smile then moved as a gravelly, cracked voice came out of him.

"Come here," he rasped.

"Come here, my ass," Reggie replied immediately as she backed away faster.

The man then took a step closer, his smile twitching more erratically. "I said come here," he growled.

Reggie had seen enough in this city to know that the homeless, drug-addled, or drunk were not to be toyed with.

"Hey, mister, look," she said, trying to quell any situation. "I don't know what your scene is, but don't do anything stupid. Okay? Just walk away."

But this man was pretty far from okay. He growled as he took more unsteady steps toward her, his expression unhinged.

As she stepped backward, she looked around frantically, looking for something to help her escape. Worried that if she just turned and ran, this man would probably be faster. She had seen a crackhead overtake a car on Sunset Boulevard before, so one catching up to an eighteen-year-old, sleep-deprived girl hopped up on malt balls would probably be easy pickings.

She then remembered the half-empty box still in her hand.

Immediately, she threw it at the man.

She did not know what to expect, but when the box missed and landed in the alley behind him, she sighed, disappointed in herself.

Stupid, stupid, she thought.

There was only one thing for her to do. She had to try and scare him off.

"See, the thing of it is," she said, forcing a half-hearted smile, "my dad's in the Special Forces, a colonel. And he's taught me to take care of myself. You know what I'm saying?" She then raised her clenched fists in front of her. "Like, you wouldn't want me to hurt you with these dangerous weapons."

The whole proposition was laughable to her, seeing as how this man was not only clearly on some mind-altering drug—he ate raw meat out of the trash, after all—but he also outweighed her by at least a hundred pounds. Sure, he may have been blind, but that didn't seem to slow him down.

"Don't buy it, huh?" she said, lowering her fists, still backing away and matching his speed. "Okay . . . okay . . . damn."

She had no choice. None at all. She had done all her dad had taught her. The four steps to confrontation.

Try to walk away

Try to joke your way out of it

Try to threaten your way out of it

Then, and only then . . . aim for the face. Always for the face.

Number four had come. With a sudden speed, she

swung her leg up and kicked the grinning man on the side of the head, causing him to stumble. As she did, the keys fell from her grasp and onto the ground. But she had no time to grab them as he regained his balance. She leaned in and swung three consecutive punches, each landing on his face. Each landing was surprisingly hard.

With the force of her beating, he collapsed backward into a heap on the ground.

She wasted no time. She had to get the keys.

Then she did something her dad would have been furious about. She could hear him now. *Never take your eyes off the enemy. Ever.*

But that is exactly what she did.

She took her eyes off the downed man for just a second, scanning the dark alley for Larry's keys. And as she did, the grinning, twitchy man staggered to his feet. *Still* grinning, *still* twitching.

In seconds, he was upon her and grabbed her from behind. His arms wrapped around her stomach as he opened his mouth and bared his teeth. But she did not give in to this disadvantage. Instead, she threw her head back with force, smashing into the bridge of his nose. She could feel and hear the bone breaking under the impact. She then lifted both elbows and brought them down into the man's ribs. Once more, he went sprawling to the ground in a heap.

Out of breath, Reggie stared in shock at the man. Once again, he clambered up to his feet. His mindless desire to continue the fight only solidified her presumption that this was drugs.

"What are you, man, a PCP freak? Crack? What is it? Or are you just plain ol' dumb?"

Feeling her energy depleting, seeing the man stand up, acting like she hadn't just used all her best moves on him—ignoring the malted ball debacle—she knew she had to do something fast to end this.

As the man started to shamble toward her again, her eyes darted around the alley. She noticed the remnants of a wooden palette leaning against one of the dumpsters. After running over, she wrenched one of the wooden slats free and held it aloft like a baseball bat.

"You don't want this, pal!" she warned.

But the man *still* grinned, *still* twitched and *still* advanced on her.

"Motherfucker," she grimaced through gritted teeth, not wanting to do this at all. But she had no choice.

He then lunged, reaching out with an open palm, as his grin widened, roaring like a beast at her.

She quickly brought her leg up, slamming the tip of her boot right into his groin with eye-watering force. Then the wooden slat she held was swung down. Smashing into the side of his head with a loud crack, sending him careening to the floor in a heap. But, unlike the last two times, this time, he fell to the floor and did not move. The hit to the skull was enough to silence him.

Sweating and breathing very heavily, Reggie looked down at the man. Before she turned to walk away, something even stranger caught her eye. Stranger than Larry's bike still in the alley, stranger than the grinning man. Something that made her stomach twist in a way the fight hadn't.

His blood. Well, was it even blood? It seeped from his mouth onto the floor. But even in the dim light, she could tell that it was not normal. It wasn't a deep red but more like a pinky honey.

This wasn't just drugs. The pale eyes. The twitching. The pink-honey blood. That voice . . . *What the hell could do that to someone?*

Looking around, she could not hide the sudden relief as she spotted the keys, which were lying on the ground less than five feet away.

Within moments, she had the keys, sprinted away from the man, and was straddling Larry's motorcycle. With the throttle twisted, she kick-started the bike in one motion. The engine started immediately with a throaty roar.

Turning to make sure of no surprises, she saw the man was still in a heap. Bleeding his weird blood. No movements at all.

She didn't hang around. As the bike lurched forward, she pulled a slight wheelie and sped out of the alley. Getting as far away from the man as fast as she could and, unbeknownst to her, far away from the remains of Larry, who she had no idea about.

As she rode through the deserted streets, the motorcycle's engine was the only sound in the otherwise creepy silence. The city, usually deafening with noise, was a ghost town. As Reggie drove by a long bank of stores that should have been open, her reflection flickered across their darkened window displays.

She had ridden for blocks, expecting to see someone, *anyone*, step out of a doorway or some half-asleep early riser crossing the street.

Her eyes noticed the neon signs of a twenty-four-hour diner, the kind of place that was always open, just as it advertised. Yet, inside, despite the lights still glowing, the booths and counter stools still stood perfectly arranged, without a single customer or worker in sight. It was open but deserted.

Was there an evacuation warning she had missed? That's all she could presume. A nuclear war broke out when she was asleep in the projection room? Was this even real? Was she dreaming? Hallucinating?

She slowed slightly as her eyes swept the streets around her. She could not believe there was no one.

It wasn't like a nighttime quiet. It was devoid of every kind of sound. It was oppressive and uncomfortable.

At an intersection, the traffic light automatically flicked to red as she approached. From force of habit, she rolled to a stop, one foot hitting the pavement to steady the bike.

She looked each way up the intersecting street.

Nothing.

Her gaze drifted farther, past the rows of parked cars to the ones that weren't parked. The ones that were scattered across the streets. Abandoned vehicles, not crashed. Not broken down, just stopped in place. Left.

And then she saw something even more unnerving.

The clothes.

Piles of them. Everywhere.

A jacket here, a pair of sneakers there. Whole outfits, shirts, pants, even sunglasses, left in individually crumpled heaps along the sidewalks and in the middle of the street.

A cold shiver crawled up her spine.

The traffic light ahead of her remained red. A ridiculous concept, considering there was no one else around to obey it.

She let out a slow breath, shifting her grip on the handlebars.

She peered up at the skyline, at the high-rise apartment blocks that loomed up, expecting maybe—*just maybe*—she would see a figure standing at a window, staring back at her. But the buildings just stood over her, silent and empty.

With a small shake of her head, she let out a short, melancholic chuckle, more disbelief than amusement.

"This is seriously fucked up," she mumbled as her fingers tensed around the clutch lever.

Not even looking at the useless traffic light, Reggie dropped the bike into gear.

As she rode her bike into the distance, heading back home, back to Sam—and, yes, even back to that evil witch Doris—she left in her wake the roar of the motorcycle. A roar that soon dissipated and vanished as if it were never there.

CHAPTER
THREE

As Reggie stepped across the grass, she felt a sinking feeling that almost made her vomit. It was the strewn clothes she had seen on her way home. The sheer amount of them.

From outside the El Rey, on Wilshire Boulevard, across fifteen miles of peopleless roads to her house in Sherman Oaks, the small, abandoned piles were everywhere. And they weren't just random. Trousers, shirts, dresses. Police uniforms. Each pile was small and individual as if the people wearing them had simply . . . vanished. She had half expected to run into a band of thousands of naked people running away, but there was nothing. No one.

Even in her own neighborhood, across her own front yard, these piles of clothes were abundant, just as they were in the streets. Just like everywhere . . .

. . . It was about then that she realized that the people did not simply take off clothes and walk away.

Where each pile stood was where the person had disappeared from. The clothes were all that was left.

She saw the Yvonne St Lawrence white pantsuit among the others.

A dull throb behind her eyes pulsed in time with the ache in her head. Stress, exhaustion, fear, panic . . . She didn't have time to dwell. She just had to keep on moving, to find out what was happening. To find Sam.

From inside the house, she could hear faint music being played. Tinny and distant.

Hesitating at the front door, her fingers fumbled as she pulled out her house keys. Realizing her hands were shaking, she took a moment to close her eyes and breathe.

Hold it together. Hold it together. Hold it together.

Opening her eyes again, not allowing any panic to surface, not yet, she stared through the frosted glass, hoping to see movement beyond. But it revealed nothing but stillness, no sign of life.

She swallowed hard, leaned in, and listened.

Just the music.

Slowly and as silently as possible, she slid the key into the lock and turned it.

It didn't budge.

Because the door was already unlocked.

That's not right, she thought. Doris never left the door unlocked. The woman double-checked the locks twice every night, convinced someone was waiting to break in and steal her jewelry—or worse, her liquor.

Her pulse sped up as she grabbed the handle and pushed it ever so slightly. The door gave way easily, creaking open. The corridor inside was dark, with the only light coming in from the other windows in the house.

Reggie stepped back and took a long, steadying breath. Forcing the pain in her head away as well as the swell of nausea in her stomach. What if there were people in the house waiting? What if the conspiracy nut were right? What if . . . *Aliens*?!

She lifted her boot and kicked the door fully open.

The door slammed into the corridor wall with an echoing thud, revealing . . . absolutely nothing untoward. She stood there, framed by the bright haze behind her. She didn't step in immediately. Instead, she lingered.

In a voice just above a whisper, she called out, "Samantha? . . . Doris?"

After this morning, after Larry's disappearance, after the pale-eyed man, after the city emptied like a ghost town, she wasn't taking any chances. She expected whatever could be hiding in her house would rush out at her after hearing her voice. She was ready to fight.

Slowly, she stepped inside, fists up. Peering into the living room as she passed. Then the kitchen. Nothing.

"Sam?" she said again cautiously.

Turning up the stairs, she followed the sound of the music. Reaching the landing, she realized the sound was coming from her sister's room, beyond the partially opened door ahead of her.

As she stepped closer, she saw the radio through the gap in the door, a small portable device sitting on

Sam's dressing table. It was playing at almost maximum volume, deafening, with its warbling reception.

Reggie stepped inside, pushing the door open slowly.

"Sam?" she said again, slightly louder.

Not that it could be heard well over the noise of the music currently being hurled at her.

Suddenly, from the other side of the door, Samantha's face popped out, staring at her, looking confused.

"What d'ya want?" she practically shouted over the music.

Ordinarily, this would not have been too startling for Reggie, but given the situation and the tension she had felt, it caused her to yelp as she staggered backward, tripped over the pair of boots, and fell onto the bed.

There, standing in front of the mirror by her closet, Samantha Belmont was dressed in her blue-and-pink Ridgemont High cheerleader uniform, her team's name *Rebels* emblazoned across the chest.

She had showered. Gotten ready. Without a clue of the things Reggie had witnessed. And there she stood, staring, wide-eyed, startled by her sister's sudden intrusion.

For a moment, they just stared at each other.

Then, as if nothing had happened, Samantha walked over and dialed the volume on the radio down.

"God, what are you trying to do, give me a damn heart attack?" she muttered, shaking her head.

She picked up a hairbrush and resumed fixing her

hair like it was the most important thing in the world to do right then.

Reggie sat up, staring in confusion.

The world had ended.

And Samantha was doing her hair.

Reggie rubbed her temples as she shook her head. "Oh, for fuck's sake."

Oblivious, Samantha kept brushing. "I thought you were Doris. You know, after your call last night, she decked me out? Punch right to the kisser. Swear she knocked one of my teeth loose."

Reggie struggled to process what any of this had to do with what had happened to the city.

But her sister kept going.

"Wait till Daddy hears about it." She jabbed a finger at her braces. "Three thousand bucks for my teeth, and Doris goes and slugs me?" She spun dramatically. "And get this—she and Chuck spent the night together. Had a drunken party and left me home alone. Oh, Daddy's gonna love that. He might even divorce her."

"What are you talking about?" Reggie asked.

Samantha checked her reflection one last time, grabbed her radio, and breezed past Reggie. Still talking. Still acting like nothing had happened.

"I ran away last night after she slugged me," she said casually, reaching the kitchen and opening the fridge. "Left a note and everything . . . so polite of me. Then I realized I had nowhere to go. So, I crashed in the storage shed."

"The shed?"

Samantha rummaged through the fridge, finally

grabbing a small leftover party sandwich from one of
the untouched platters.

She took a bite. "Yeah, it was pretty gross in there,"
she said, chewing. "Slug pellets, trash bags full of dead
leaves, smelled like baked assholes . . ." She thought for
a moment, shivering visibly at how gross she remembered it was. "But I figured *whatever*. I'd just go to
squad practice in the morning and then run away after.
No point missing it just because of Doris, right?
Thought I could crash at friends' places 'til Daddy gets
back."

Reggie could only look at her sister in surprise.

"Except . . ." Samantha frowned as she licked a
crumb off her thumb. "I don't know if practice is even
on today. I can't get anybody on the phone. Tried to call
for a lift . . . But . . . No one is picking up."

She shrugged, popped the last of the sandwich in
her mouth, and chewed.

Finally given a chance to talk, Reggie stepped in
closer. "Sammy," she said with urgency. "You can't get
anyone on the phone because they're all gone . . . Everybody's gone!"

Samantha blinked. "Huh?"

Reggie's frustration quickly boiled over. She
grabbed Samantha by the shoulders, shaking her.

"There is nobody!" she said. "Swear to God . . . not a
single fucking person! No one! Nada! Zilch. Zero.
None!"

Samantha smiled, nodding along, as if Reggie had
just told her some elaborate joke. "Right. Yeah, sure.
Nobody."

With a flash of annoyance, Reggie turned and walked to the front door, pulling Samantha along with her by the sleeve. "Come here."

"Hey, back off!" Samantha complained. "This sweater cost eighty bucks!"

Out of the kitchen, through the front door and onto the lawn, Reggie dragged Samantha, yelling. "Look! Look at all this!"

Pulling out of Reggie's grip, Samantha looked around the cul-de-sac with annoyed confusion, rubbing her sore arm.

"Look at what? So, they didn't clean up?"

Reggie shook her head, pointing to the clothes.

But Samantha was having none of it. "What's your beef? The sky is red? So? It's a shit tip out here? What? You're acting like the world ended or something!"

"Sammy . . ." Reggie grimaced. "I . . ." She paused. "Doris *isn't* at Chuck's!"

"Huh? What do you mean? Of course she is."

Reggie locked eyes with her sister. She wasn't playing around. "You wanna see her?"

Samantha thought for a quick beat before sneering. "Not particularly."

Reggie walked over to the grass and pointed to the white crumpled pantsuit she had noticed on the way in.

"Here!" she said, stooping down and picking up Doris's cheap clothes. "This is Doris." As she did, from out of the fabric, a fine red dust fell to the floor. Grimacing, she dropped the clothes back onto the grass. "That is all that's left of her, of all of them!"

Reggie noticed another pile of clothes next to her. A

beige cargo jacket, black T-shirt, pants, white loafers, and . . .

She hesitated before crouching, then reached for the tangled dark mane that was half-sprawled on the pile. Her fingers brushed the strands, and she let out a brief, humorless laugh. "Huh," she murmured, picking up Chuck's wig and holding it up to Samantha. "Guess you were right, Sammy. Wasn't his real hair after all." She turned it over as the grim reality settled in quickly, and she let it fall back down. Facing Samantha, she expected a snarky remark, but all she got was silence.

Samantha just stood still, her face pale, her eyes staring at the empty clothes. Unsure of how to process any of it.

It didn't make sense. It *couldn't* make sense.

Her first instinct was to laugh—not because it was funny but because it was impossible.

"This is a joke, right?" Samantha said, forcing an uneasy chuckle. "I mean, come on. Where's the hidden camera? Did Doris finally get some weird sense of humor and decide to screw with me?"

Reggie didn't answer.

Samantha swallowed hard, eyes darting around the yard like she expected Doris to jump out from behind a bush at any second, smirking, drink in hand, telling her to stop being such a brat.

She looked back at the clothes and the red dust.

A queasy feeling settled deep in her gut.

"No," she muttered, shaking her head as she took a step back. "No, she . . . she probably just, like . . . I don't know, ran off naked or something. Wouldn't be the first time she embarrassed herself."

Reggie exhaled sharply. "Sammy, think. Does that sound even remotely normal?"

Samantha wasn't listening. She couldn't. Her hands clenched at her sides, breath coming too fast, too uneven.

"Or maybe it's . . . it's like some kind of ruse," she continued, voice a little too high, too forced. "Like in the movies, you know? Where they fake their own death? Maybe she and Chuck just . . . just skipped town. Maybe they're in Vegas right now, laughing their asses off—"

She didn't believe the words coming out of her mouth. There was not just her and Chuck's clothes here but everyone's who were at the party.

When she turned away from the lawn, she pressed a hand to her temple like that would stop the static roar of panic.

Reggie softened, stepping forward. "Sammy, you okay?"

"I just need a second," Samantha whispered.

She didn't wait for a response. She turned on her heel and walked inside.

Reggie gave one last glance at Doris's hollow, fabric remains, then sighed.

She followed her sister.

A few minutes later, they were back in the kitchen, and Samantha was pulling the milk from the fridge and a box of Raisin Bran from the cabinet. She needed some normality. She had that sandwich, but this wasn't about eating but about regaining some hold of the morning. The morning that was quickly spinning out of control.

On the portable radio, a song was playing softly in the background. Not that she was paying it any attention. She couldn't. She was too locked in on the ludicrousness of the situation.

She poured the cereal into a bowl, then the milk, barely aware of what she was doing.

Behind her, Reggie was looking worriedly at her sister. She knew she'd handled this badly, coming in at her too hard, too fast. She should have eased her into the information, not thrown her straight into the deep end of everyone they knew being dead. Hardly a subject you could lightheartedly just announce.

"They can't be all gone," Samantha said, her back still to Reggie. She lifted a spoonful of cereal to her mouth and took a bite, chewing slowly. "They're around. They gotta be." She swallowed her food, then added, quieter this time, "You're not funny, you know?"

Reggie crossed to the phone on the wall, lifted the receiver, and started to dial a number.

"If you're trying to scare me," Samantha added, still not turning, "you're doing a great job of it, okay? Does that make you happy?"

"I'm not trying to scare you," Reggie said as she listened to the phone for an answer but got no reply.

Samantha cracked, putting the bowl on the counter and whirling angrily to face her sister. "Then, stop it! Stop all of this! What are you trying to do?"

Reggie could not stop herself from snapping back. "*I'm* not doing a fucking thing!" she shouted, holding up the phone. "Try calling someone. Not just the Pep Squad but anyone. Absolutely anyone. *Nobody's* home!"

Samantha looked at Reggie helplessly. "But . . . how?"

Reggie attempted a kind, reassuring smile. "Well, I'm here. We got each other. Even if there is no one else."

"What did this?"

"Did you watch the comet?"

Samantha shook her head.

"Right, you were in the shed. No windows in there. I was in the theater. None there either. Must have been that."

"Where are the bodies?"

Reggie couldn't answer that.

At that moment, the song on the radio cut off, and the voice of Mighty Mike could be heard, filling the silence between the sisters. "Well, looks like we have sorted out all the technical issues earlier. Mighty Mike will never leave you in the lurch without the hot rocking tunes to start your weekend. And in the balmy City of Angels, it looks like it's going to be a great day for the beach, just like every day. It sure is gonna be a hot, hot, hot day!"

Both sisters looked at the radio and then at each other.

"He's not gone?" Samantha said quietly. "So, it's not just us?"

"Isn't that station by Skid Row? Come on, let's go. We can take Doris's car."

The drive across the city in Doris's Mercedes was a silent one.

Samantha looked out of the window as Reggie drove, navigating the empty streets ahead of her, avoiding the cars that had been abandoned in their lanes as they drove through the red-tinged city, headed to the KJJR radio station.

The traffic lights on their way kept cycling as stop signs stood at their usual corners. Storefronts glowed with neon signs advertising diners and liquor stores, but all were still empty.

Samantha's knee bounced as her hands fidgeted with the hem of her cheerleading sweatshirt. She still wasn't handling this well, not yet. Reggie could see that much. Her sister was obviously trying to mentally shove what she had seen into some kind of normal, rational box.

Reggie wondered how she had just accepted this all so calmly. She wasn't panicking. Should she be? Everyone seemed to have gone. Disintegrated as they stared at the comet. Burned to a cinder? Wait, wait, she was being too rational. Where was the panic? Where were the tears for her friends? Her family? Her neighbors? Reggie was just accepting of this new order with a relaxed ease, which disturbed her more than what had actually happened. She was her father's daughter. He would be the same. He would just move on. *No point crying over spilled milk,* as he loved to say.

Damn. Her dad. Was he gone, too? No, she had to push this thought aside. Just deal with the facts that she could. And she knew that Samantha would not be far behind. They were sisters and so similar in a lot of ways. A great ability for compartmentalization was one of them. She was just taking longer to get there.

From the car radio, Mighty Mike's voice crackled out, as confident as ever. ". . . Some sort of trouble here . . . We'll have it fixed in a second. Just hold on to whatever horses you have."

Samantha looked at the radio quizzically. Hadn't she heard him say that before?

As the song started, Mighty Mike cut in over the intro. "Okay, folks," he said enthusiastically. "Here to get you up and at them are the dulcet tones of Stallion with 'Let My Fingers Do the Talking.'"

Reggie finally exhaled. "Alright, spill," she said to her sister, stealing all attention away from the radio.

"Spill what?"

"Talk to me . . . Whatever's going on in that head of yours," Reggie said. "Because you're not arguing or talking shit, which means you're either finally believing what's happening, or you're planning to jump out of the car at the next red light. I gotta make sure we're on the same page. We are both alive, and we can cry about all this later, when we know what happened."

Samantha smiled thinly but didn't deny what was being said. Instead, she folded her arms and sank farther into the seat, staring straight ahead.

"This can't be happening, can it?" she said. "They can't have just gone just like that."

"Well, that's exactly what it looks like?" Reggie deadpanned. "You think if they were still around that Chuck would leave his wig or Doris would leave her clothes?" She realized she was unintentionally sounding annoyed. "I don't know how, but something happened last night. Something big." She shook her head. "We just need to find someone, anyone, who knows what the hell is going on. Only people I saw was a crackhead near the theater and you. So, there are some survivors, just like us. Maybe there are a lot of us? But from the looks of it, they are not in the city."

"A crackhead?"

"You don't wanna know, trust me."

"And Mighty Mike?"

Reggie sighed. "Look, if you have a better idea, I'm all ears. But he's alive."

As they crossed into downtown, a sudden burst of static from the radio made both of them jump as the signal faded, then came back in without any music and just the sound of clicking and whirring beneath an electric hum. Until the voice of Mighty Mike came back.

"I know what you're thinking, folks." His voice was barely audible through the static. "What kind of cowboy outfit is KJJR? Well, just hold tight. Normality will resume as soon as the radio Gods allow it."

The nearest available parking for the radio station was down the street in one of the paid parking lots. But with the city being like it was, Reggie had parked the Mercedes half off the curb directly in front of the building. Right where a traffic sign ineptly demanded *No Parking*.

As the two of them got out and walked through the glass doors that led into KJJR, they were hit with how cold it was inside the building. The air-conditioned stillness of an office without people to warm it up felt quite stagnant. This building would normally be alive with ringing phones, the chatter of voices, the shuffling of papers, the sound of music. But, like the city, it was deathly silent.

Reggie and Samantha stood inside the lobby, their eyes glancing over the vacant desks, the abandoned chairs and the lifeless phones. The only sound they could hear was the muffled music filtering in from further inside the building.

Samantha hesitated, hugging her arms around herself. "Do you think it happened everywhere?" she asked. Her voice was soft, almost hopeful, like she was daring Reggie to tell her no. "Like, in Burbank? Or other places? Where Daddy is?"

Reggie didn't answer. She had no answers. She didn't know.

A voice cut through the air from a nearby speaker. "Alright, sports fans! I hope you're enjoying the tunes because Mighty Mike has got you covered all day long!"

"He's here," Samantha whispered.

They quickly followed the voice, moving through

the lobby and into the station itself. As they walked down the long corridor, only the sound of their sneakers squeaking lightly on the linoleum and the music drifting down the corridor could be heard.

As they continued closer to a large door marked *Studio*, the voice of Mighty Mike had become a lot clearer. His usual over-the-top energy bounced through the speakers above the door.

"... Some sort of trouble here ... We'll have it fixed in a second. Just hold on to whatever horses you have."

"This isn't right," Samantha said. "He's said that before."

"Only one way to find out," Reggie said, lifting a hand and knocking lightly upon the studio door.

There was no answer.

The song started to play, and over the intro, Mighty Mike kept talking. "Here to get you up and at them are the dulcet tones of Stallion with 'Let My Fingers Do the Talking.'"

Samantha frowned. "Oh, come on, it's all the same stuff!"

Reggie knocked again, louder.

Instead of waiting for an answer, Samantha had enough. She rolled her eyes. "Just go in already." She shoved the door open.

Inside, the studio was bathed in the glow of blinking buttons, sliders, and computer screens. A large broadcast console sat at the center of the room, surrounded by stacks of tape carts and old-school reel-to-reel audio players. Speakers mounted on the walls pumped out the same smooth, manufactured DJ patter that had greeted them before.

But Mighty Mike wasn't there.

The chair at the console was empty. A microphone was propped in front of it.

A loud *click* suddenly echoed through the room, making them both jump.

They spun toward the source of the sound, watching as a mechanical arm pulled a tape cart from a slot and slid it into a player.

A beat.

Then from the speakers . . .

"Well, looks like we have sorted out all the technical issues earlier. Mighty Mike will never leave you in the lurch without the hot, rocking tunes to start your weekend. And in the balmy City of Angels, it looks like it's going to be a great day for the beach, just like every day. It sure is gonna be a hot, hot, hot day!"

Another *click*.

Another tape cart being loaded and sucked into the machine.

"This is a million-watt radio station. Every time something goes wrong, the Chief Engineer says, 'What?!' That happens about a million times a day."

The machine continued its automated search, rifling through tape carts, looking for something to play. When it finally found one, marked *106-TROUBLE ANNOUNCE* it loaded it into the player, and within moments, music started to sound again, rolling on, as though nothing had happened.

The whole system was on autopilot.

"Told you I heard it before!" Samantha said.

"Son of a bitch," Reggie moaned.

"Where is he, then?"

Before Reggie could answer, another voice spoke.

"Well, surprise, surprise."

Both girls spun around to where the voice came from, barely stifling their screams.

There, in the shadows, by the doorway, was a man. In his hand, he held a Saturday Night Special. One of those compact, small-caliber pistols made from low-quality metal.

A tall, broad-shouldered man in his early twenties. His dark hair was slightly unkempt, and he looked tired yet disguised it behind a very cocksure attitude. He wore a frayed dark denim jacket with a red T-shirt underneath. He had on his face a look of casual amusement. The gun in his hand was held toward them. But not aimed, just pointed in their general direction . . . for now.

"How's it goin'?" he said as if they'd just run into each other at the grocery store.

Reggie and Samantha's eyes flicked between his annoyingly handsome face and the weapon.

"First thing I want you to do . . ." he said, tilting the gun slightly, "is to come a little closer." He pointed his gun at Samantha. "You first."

Before she could stop herself, Reggie took a slow step forward, blurting, "Look . . . just let my sister go, okay? After she's gone, maybe we can work something out."

"Hey!" Samantha's head snapped toward her. "I'm not going anywhere!"

"Shhh!" Reggie hissed.

The man chuckled, shaking his head. "You got the wrong idea, Big Sis."

His grip on the gun didn't change, but something in his posture shifted . . . less tense, more at ease.

"Now," he continued, "I'm gonna give you five seconds. One . . . two . . . three—"

"Okay, okay!" Samantha said as she took a step closer to him. "Jeez, if this is how you get off!"

He quickly reached out, grabbed her arm, and pulled her the rest of the way toward him.

"Leave her alone!" Reggie barked as she went on the attack, but he quickly aimed his gun straight at her face, stopping her in her tracks.

"I told you this isn't what you think," he reiterated, a nervous waver in his voice. "Keep calm, okay?"

Letting go of Samantha's arm, the man yanked her head back into the light cast by the automatic playback machines, keeping his aim on Reggie. He looked into Samantha's eyes. Checking each one.

With a satisfied nod, he quickly let her go, ushering her back toward Reggie. "C'mon, Big Sis. Your turn."

Samantha wasn't even angry, only confused.

"You gotta let me see your eyes," he ordered. "That's all."

Taking a cautious step nearer, Reggie tilted her head to the light for him to see.

Leaning closer, he quickly let out a sigh of relief.

"Okay," he said, lowering his gun. "I'm sorry, but I had to be sure."

"Sure of what?" Samantha asked.

He continued. "I know what you're thinking—"

"That you're a prick?" Reggie asked.

He smirked. "You guys come in here looking like Clairol ads," he said. He motioned toward the door. "I dunno if you've seen those freaked-out albinos running around out there, but I had to make sure you weren't one of 'em. They all got those white eyes."

"Freaked out what now?" Samantha asked.

But Reggie already knew what he meant.

"I was jumped by one outside work. There's more?"

Samantha turned to her. "Wait, what? The crack-head? He jumped you?"

"'Cause of Larry . . . he . . . he disappeared. And one of those guys, whatever was wrong with him . . . showed up. Tried to get me, but I knocked him clean out."

"You didn't think that was important to mention to me?"

Reggie opened her mouth but hesitated. "I . . . I didn't want to scare you."

Samantha let out a sharp breath, shaking her head. "So, instead, you bring me to a radio station where we almost get shot by this asshole?"

The man laughed. "Well, you're lucky you got away, but there's not that many of them. I've seen about four, and I've been all over the city. But they are dangerous." He thought for a second. "And to be clear, I wasn't gonna shoot you unless you were one of them . . . Besides, I'm not an asshole. The name's Hector. Hector Gomez . . . Pleasure to meet ya both. And in answer to your question—no, I don't work here."

"Of course you don't," Reggie said.

"I drive a truck. I was heading to San Diego with this hitchhiker, this girl. I had to stop for gas, so I pulled in downtown and . . . I saw one of those pale fuckers . . . They were eatin' a cat."

Samantha wrinkled her nose. "A *dead* cat?"

Hector shook his head. "Semi-dead at best."

Reggie ignored the cat part. "What happened to the girl?"

Hector's casual facade slipped just for a second. "She freaked out when she saw it, took off running." His voice went quieter. "I saw her about twenty minutes later. Two of those things had . . . torn her apart." He swallowed. "Literally . . . into pieces."

Both girls fell silent.

"Both of them were eating her," Hector continued. "Like full-on fuckin' *Night of the Living Dead*. They're definitely zombies. But I saw it all. And she didn't come back. So, these zombies can't make others, I guess."

"Oh, no," Reggie muttered as a silent realization washed over her. "Larry."

But before anyone could ask her what was wrong, Reggie was already backing away, her hand clamping over her mouth as she bolted from the studio, the door slamming shut behind her.

"Who's Larry?" Hector asked.

"This guy she hangs out with—" Samantha scanned

the studio with a sudden look of concern. "Hang on—how safe is that place?"

"Safe enough. I checked it all out."

"Safe enough my ass. You left both front doors unlocked. How do you think we got in? You should have this place locked up! You're lucky we locked them behind us."

Hector smiled. "And that is why I'm a truck driver and not in charge of the nation's defense."

In the KJJR washroom, Reggie leaned over the sink, gripping the edges as she tried to steady herself, staring at her reflection in the mirror. Her face was pale, her eyes red-rimmed. The taste of bile lingered in her mouth, a gross reminder of the malted milk balls she had lost to the toilet bowl moments earlier.

She yanked a paper towel from a nearby dispenser and ran it under cold water before pressing it against her face.

Her thoughts were stuck on Larry. Was that his blood back in the alley? Was he still alive when she rode off on his bike? Could she have saved him from . . . that thing? And zombies? Did the comet vaporize the city but left zombies? How? How does that make sense?

She realized that, in all likelihood, she would never be able to make sense of this. She was not a scientist and had no way of knowing anything for sure. She had discounted the hordes of naked people who abandoned their clothes only because she hadn't seen any . . . when, in reality, they could've been out there.

She made a silent pact to herself. She would just take everything as it happened. The why and how were no longer attainable. She just had to survive. She just had to protect herself and Sam.

These thoughts wouldn't stop spinning in her head, looping over and over again.

After a couple of minutes, the washroom door creaked open.

Reggie tensed as she saw Hector in the mirror. He lingered in the doorway, leaning in from outside, a bottle of scotch dangling from his hand.

"Hey," he said, lifting the bottle to her. "Wanna drink? Might help. Always helps me!"

"Please leave me alone."

"I'm just trying to be nice."

"Oh, I'm charmed, I'm sure," she said quietly, wiping her mouth with the moist towel.

Hector rolled his eyes, shifting his weight. "Look, don't take your shit out on me, okay? None of this is my fault, you know. Lil' Sis seems to be handling it a hell of a lot better than you."

Annoyed, Reggie turned to face him. "Don't you call her that."

Hector raised an eyebrow. "What? Lil' Sis?"

"She's got a name," Reggie said coolly. "And it's *not* that."

Hector smirked. "Kinda hard to call her by her name when none of you have even told me what it is."

He had a point.

Reggie opened her mouth but hesitated. "Samantha. She's called Samantha."

"And you?"

"My friends call me Reggie," she replied flatly. "So, I guess that means you can call me Regina."

Hector chuckled. "Well, Regina, Samantha's handling this better than you. You should try to relax. Not like we can change shit about shit."

"It's only because she hasn't really seen what's going on. She's only been out of her house for about an hour."

"And you've seen it all, I suppose?"

She placed the moist towel in the trash can as she tried to work out her thoughts. "This much I can tell," she said. "Whatever's happening, it isn't just happening around here. It must be linked to the comet, so anywhere that people saw the comet, this had to have happened. That's just logic. You know that, right? So that means, as logic dictates, that this is *everywhere*, at least on this side of the world. I have no idea if people in China would have seen the comet at all. But we cannot assume that. We just gotta think it's everyone. And, as for Sammy, she thinks our dad is gonna come back from Honduras with the Navy Seals or something. To save the day."

"She could be right. You never know."

Reggie quickly changed the subject, still trying to clarify the situation of how Hector was here. "If you were driving a truck, how come you're here? You would have seen the comet too, right?"

With a sly smirk, Hector explained. "Me and that girl . . . We pulled off the road for the night. Spent the evening in the back of my truck. No windows in there.

And we found enough to distract us from the thunder that comet made. No need to see fireworks if you're getting fireworks, if you know what I mean?"

Reggie looked at him with unimpressed disapproval.

"Hey, comet or no comet," he laughed. "I'd been on the road for three weeks, and the opportunity just presented itself. Who am I to say no?"

In the radio station studio, Samantha sat behind the broadcast console, staring at the microphone that hung in front of her. This console was a sea of blinking buttons, each glowing at her in a different color.

She smiled at the biggest button of all . . . the glaring red one. One that said *AIR* in big letters on it.

"Fuck it," she mumbled, pressing it down.

Immediately, there was a sound of a clank followed by a mechanical whirr as the automated arm halted, cutting off the looped tapes. The machine powered down with a final click, and a red light flared to life on the wall in front of her. *ON AIR.*

"Oh, hell to the fuck yeah." She grinned, clearly impressed by it. Clearing her throat, she leaned forward to the microphone.

"Testing. Testing, One, two, three, four, five. Once, I caught a fish alive. This is your host, the awesome, the beautiful, your supreme queen, Samantha Belmont speaking, now one-third owner of the greater Los Angeles basin."

She glanced at the telephone that sat next to the

console, at the sign that said HIT LINE above it, with the printed script to read out below.

"Call the KJJR Hit Line on 555-4487—that's 555-HITS. Call up now, and we can get your hits a-rollin'."

The tension between Hector and Reggie had settled . . . at least for now. They both sat on the floor of the bathroom, backs against the wall, the scotch bottle having been opened and partially drunk.

Reggie had Hector's handgun, turning it over with the practiced ease of someone who knew exactly what she was doing. She checked the weight, tested the slide, and inspected the barrel. Her fingers moved with expertise that didn't match her age or look.

Hector, watching her, raised an eyebrow at this.

"How much did you pay for this, a couple of bucks?" she asked, unimpressed.

Hector smiled, resting his arms on his knees. "That's a twenty-dollar article. Only one I could afford."

Reggie let out a low whistle, shaking her head as she popped the barrel and peered at the bullets inside. "Well, it may be okay for date night in the barrio," she said dryly, sliding it back in with a click. "But if we run up against any more of those guys outside, we're gonna need some real firepower."

"You know, for someone who was about to puke their guts out five minutes ago, you sure bounce back fast."

Reggie didn't look at him. "I've had worse mornings," she muttered, absentmindedly flipping the safety on and off. "But, seriously . . . if this is all you've got, we may as well be throwing rocks."

Samantha was fully into her new self-appointed role as a DJ. She had figured out how to play music, thanks to the mixing desk's obvious labeling. As the song ended on the turntable, she pushed the fader from *MUSIC* to *TALK*. Lifting the needle off the record, she turned back to the microphone.

"Okay, my little teenage comet zombies . . . that was . . . I have no idea, just the first record I could find." Lifting the disc off the turntable, she read the label aloud. "Seems that was the band the Misfits, with a lovely song called 'Last Caress,' which was a bit loud for me, personally . . . Anyway, here are some changes to the scheduled programming of our lives . . . Most of you guys had finals starting next week, right? Well, guess what? They're called off. I can also proclaim a new rule to my loyal subjects . . . The legal drinking age is ten, but you will need ID. No *ifs*, no *buts*, and absolutely *no* tantrums at the bar. We run a tight ship of chaos here, people." She could not stop smiling at her joke. "And if any of you wanna hear a song, I'm, of course, still taking requests . . . I will—"

One of the lights on the Hit Line telephone suddenly started to flash, and her expression dropped.

"You know the Armed Forces Reserve Center in Los Alamitos?" Reggie said to Hector as she passed his gun back to him. "Well, my dad used to take us there for target practice. They've got automatic weapon storage."

"You know how to use those things?" he asked, looking unsurely at her as he motioned to his gun. "I barely know how to use *this*."

"Come on," she laughed. "The Uzi nine-millimeter submachine gun was practically designed for house-wives. Anyone can use one."

Before he could laugh, the door to the washroom was flung open as Samantha came bursting in. She was screaming and on the verge of happy tears. Barely able to get the words out.

"I got a call!" she said in a fluster. "Someone's trying to rescue us! An old dude in the desert or something."

Reggie and Hector immediately sprang to their feet.

"Who? What?" he asked in shock.

"I don't know! I was messing about on the radio!"

Rushing into the studio in a near panic, Samantha pointed to the phone on the console that was laying off the hook.

"The call came in on the hit line," she said. "I was just playing about. Guy said he was part of a big group."

Hector walked over and grabbed the phone. "Hel-lo?" he said, hoping against all hope that people were there.

"They're not there," Samantha added. "The line went dead."

"Dead?" He repeated, the phone still to his ear. "What do you mean dead?"

With all the furor, the emotion and excitement of the call was getting too much for Samantha. She fought back the tears that were building. The joy that all may be okay.

"Hey, what do you mean?" Hector persisted. "Did they say they were coming?"

"I don't know."

Samantha's voice cracked as the tears started to run.

"For Christ's sake, think," he added with some unintended aggression.

"Hey," Reggie stepped in, facing him. "Shut up. You don't talk to her like that!"

Samantha's tears were turning hysterical, and the floodgates opened. The emotion she felt even from last night's confrontation with Doris, on top of all the horrors they were going through, had been forced to the forefront by this phone call.

Hector shook his head. "Sorry, but this ain't the time for her to go Looney Tunes."

"They said they were in the desert," Samantha blubbed, trying to maintain her breathing and stop more unwelcome tears.

"What desert?" Reggie asked. "Where?"

"I don't know," Samantha whined.

"Fuckin' perfect," Hector moaned. "You speak to people who could help, and you don't know shit."

"Hey, asshole," Reggie sneered. "How about you point your cheap-ass gun on her again? Maybe you can scare it out of her."

Samantha wasn't with this conversation, just caught in the emotion. "Maybe they'll call back," she suggested softly.

Those words made the tension come to an end as Hector looked at the phone receiver still in his hand. He suddenly realized that no one could call back as long as the phone was not on the cradle. He quickly replaced it.

They all watched the Hit Line phone, expecting, hoping, praying for it to suddenly ring and for all their troubles to be over.

CHAPTER
FOUR

CARTER, a stern-looking man in his fifties, grimaced as he ran a hand through his graying hair and then slammed the phone onto the table. The clunk echoed loudly, but the scientists around him barely reacted, their faces all resigned. The sterile room, something between a hospital and a lab, hummed with machinery. Fluorescent lights reflected off metal surfaces and identical uniforms.

"I can't get through," he said, controlling his annoyance. "The phone's gone dead."

Oscar, a younger stout man, sat at a large table and leaned back with an air of resignation. "I think the public utilities are going to become less and less dependable as more and more systems fail."

Carter thought for a moment. "If they stay put, we can still get them. We *have* to get them."

Wilson, a man in his thirties who was desperately trying to appear older—hence the pipe he kept clamped between his teeth—nodded thoughtfully. "From a psychological standpoint, the radio station would represent a link to normalcy. They probably wouldn't wander far as long as it was operating. Had power. AC. Access to food."

Audrey, the only one in the room who felt like she had any intellect left in this discussion, folded her arms. She was sharp, businesslike, and not one to waste words.

"Dr. Carter," she said. "I'd like to say upfront that I'm opposed to this. We shouldn't be doing any of it. No matter the personal consequences."

Carter turned to her with a look of disapproval. "And what about the disintegration? Are we supposed to just stand back and let it happen? You could live with that? This is the greater good, not teatime with small-minded morals!"

Audrey stood her ground. "We don't know that the condition is progressive. This is just all guesswork we've done with the *very* limited data at hand."

Oscar shook his head. "I think we've established that it *is* progressive, Audrey." His voice was patient but tired. "Total exposure resulted in almost immediate disintegration of the tissue. Partial protection seems to result in a proportionate slowing of the overall effect, but progression is steady in any and every case we've seen. Drying of the body fluids, a transition stage, a mindless craving to get those fluids by any means . . . and finally, calcium dust."

The group fell into an uneasy silence. A few of them

shot glances at Audrey, the only dissenting voice in the room. She knew she was outnumbered, but that didn't make her any less right in her mind.

"But we don't even know if the transfusions will work," she pressed. "This is all a waste of our valuable time and resources, based on supposition and hope, which—if I may add—are the enemies of science."

Carter's expression didn't soften. "Let me get this crystal clear in my mind. Would you have us not even try? Just sit back and wait?"

Audrey dropped her gaze to the floor, knowingly hiding her gritted jaw. She had no answer, not one they really wanted to hear, anyway.

Carter turned his attention back to the other more agreeable scientists. "We don't want to end up in the city after dark, as we have seen that is when the infected come out. And we need twenty-twenty vision on this. We'll go in tomorrow." He hesitated. "We've also had some indication of survivors in San Bernardino, Las Vegas, and Stockton. But who knows their condition? We will start with Los Angeles first, as they seem, from initial contact, clean of all effects. So far."

At that, Audrey sighed loudly and purposefully. She then turned and walked out of the room, her exit punctuated by the loud slam of the door shutting behind her.

Mostly masked behind the haze, the sun, seemingly larger than usual, burned a deep, smoldering orange. It dipped beyond the city skyline as shadows stretched long across the empty streets. The haze was streaked with crimson and violet as the last remnants of light clung stubbornly before finally surrendering to the night.

And as if nothing had changed, the city came alive . . . as much as it could. Automated systems, programmed to flicker to life at sundown, switched on without an audience. Neon signs buzzed and flickered. A row of chaser lights sputtered on, blinking in an endless loop around the entrance of a seedy adult club. They beckoned, advertised, oblivious to the fact that there was no one left to see them.

From one of the city's vacant streets, a roar of an engine could be heard approaching. A rising wail of a Porsche tore through the quiet. The sound bounced off the surrounding buildings, filling the space where the sound of nightlife should have been.

As the sports car sped around the corner and down the long empty stretch of Sunset Boulevard, it zigzagged effortlessly around the occasional abandoned vehicles left on the road.

In the driver's seat, Samantha gripped the wheel with one hand, the other wrapped around a half-drunk can of beer. She took a long swig as her eyes flicked to the rearview then back to the road ahead.

She was not the crying girl from before. She was determined and rebellious.

"They're not gonna blame me because that damn phone went dead," she mumbled to herself, her words slightly slurring from the effects of the alcohol.

"Samantha," she mimicked in a whining tone, mocking Hector and Reggie, "why didn't you do this? Why did the phone cut out? What, did you not suddenly know the inner workings of the damn universe?" Her voice was quickly replaced by her own grimace. "I'm not the stupid phone company. *Nobody* is. Not anymore."

The Porsche shot through a deserted intersection, and the red light that tried to stop her was powerless as she passed.

The city was hers, the roads open and endless. She could drive where she wanted as fast as she wanted in whoever's car she wanted. She didn't need a license or permission or to obey any of the rules of the road. Who would stop her?

Something then happened that made her stomach drop and almost swerved the car off the road.

The moment she passed the intersection doing sixty, a darkened vehicle that stood in a dark side street suddenly sprang to life. Its headlights snapped on, and it sped out onto the street in pursuit.

Then came its red-and-blue flashing lights, with the wail of the siren. The police siren.

Samantha gasped as she caught the approaching reflection in her mirror.

"What the hell?!" she blurted, whipping her head around to confirm what she saw in the mirror. The police car was closing in fast, its lights cutting through the darkening night.

"Where the fuck were you guys earlier?" she snapped to herself, exasperated.

Instinct took over as did her fear of getting in any real trouble.

They would understand, right? Especially in these circumstances.

More importantly, why was anyone policing an abandoned city at the end of the world?

She soon dropped her speed and eased the Porsche toward the curb, slowing to a stop.

The siren blared and lights flashed as the police cruiser pulled up directly behind her.

Her hands scrambled for her purse, instinctively reaching for a license she didn't even have. She had totally forgotten . . . she'd never taken the test, never even owned a car. Years of watching movies had ingrained the habit: reach for your license, hand over your registration. But this wasn't even her car. She stole it. Not that anyone was left to care.

"Oh, shit," she groaned.

Another realization quickly hit.

She looked down at the can of beer still clutched in her hand.

"Oh, double shit!"

Heart pounding, she looked around the car for a place to stash the can. She could hear the cruiser's doors opening behind her, followed by the heavy thud of boots hitting the pavement.

They were getting closer.

"Fuckity fucksticks," she hissed as she found no good place to put it. In a sudden desperation, she jammed the can behind her back, pressing it against the seat, then quickly cupped a hand over her mouth, exhaling heavily to check her breath.

It was not great. She could smell the reek of beer quite easily.

Behind her, two officers had gotten out of the police cruiser and were standing at the Porsche, one on either side.

Samantha forced a smile, trying her best to appear casual as she wound down the window. "I know you're probably gonna give me a ticket or something," she said, her voice light, "but I'm really glad to see you guys. Where were you hiding?"

She couldn't see the officer's face, so she leaned in for a better look. The moment she did, he suddenly ducked his head, revealing it.

Samantha's breath caught in her throat.

The uniform was right, but the man inside it was anything but. His face was horrifying. His lips, unnaturally red, curled back to reveal a mouth lined with jagged fangs. His skin was rotten and dripping off his bones. His eyes were glowing bright white as he opened his mouth and let out a terrifying roar.

Samantha screamed herself awake.

Jolting upward, she looked around to get her bearings. She was lying on the couch in the executive office of the KJJR radio station. For a moment, she remained still, her mind struggling to shake off the lingering traces of the nightmare. Wiping a hand across her forehead, she willed herself to calm down.

The dark office soon came into focus as her eyes adjusted to the gloom. Reggie was slouched in a large chair across from her, asleep. Each exhalation let out a light snore.

Pushing herself off the couch and to her feet, Samantha's body felt heavy and just as exhausted as it was. Without another glance at her sister, she moved toward the door and slipped out.

The corridor was quiet except for the faint music from the automated show still playing in the studio. They had chosen to start up the repeating broadcast again, favoring the banality of Mighty Mike and the same songs, over the silence of dead air.

Samantha made no sound as she walked over to the bathroom. The door creaked softly as she pulled it shut behind her. The lights inside flickered on, activated by her movement.

Walking over to the mirror, she looked at her reflection. She was pale and very much over all this whole apocalypse.

Turning on the faucet, she let the water run cold before cupping her hands beneath the stream and splashing some on her face. Forcing herself awake and shaking off the bad dreams once and for all.

She was too warm. Much too warm.

Taking off her cheerleader sweater, she draped it over the nearby paper towel dispenser. Keeping it off the tiled floor. Then, sluggishly, she unfastened her skirt and put it with her sweater, leaving her standing in nothing but her underwear.

She turned the faucet to hot, grabbed a wad of paper

towels, and began to soak them under the warm stream. She knew how much she stank. The day had brought on many sweaty nerves, and without any deodorant with her, she favored a sink wash over sitting in her own stench.

The moment the damp cloth touched her skin, something moved from one of the stalls behind her.

A massive, hairy hand lunged. Before she could react or see it in the mirror, it grabbed her, yanking her to one side.

The room spun, vision tilted as she was slammed against the wall. A panic exploded inside her as she struggled against the grip clasped around her throat, strangling any screams from her.

The thing that held her was wearing a police uniform.

And its face, its grotesque, twisted face, was straight from her nightmare.

This monster cop sneered grotesquely. "This is for your stepmom, you little punk," it said in a sickly tone.

She did not even see the large flick knife in its hand as it was driven into her, just beneath her rib cage. The blade split through her guts as it was then yanked upward, cutting clean through her intestines and into her lungs.

"FUCK!" Samantha screamed in terror as she scrambled up from the couch, her body covered with sweat.

She was back in the executive office as her scream echoed around the room. She could still feel the blade tearing through her insides, could still feel the copper taste of her own blood in her throat. Her pulse hammered loudly in her ears as her eyes darted around the room wildly, trying to separate the nightmare from reality.

Reggie had shot up from her chair, woken suddenly by her sister's panic. At the same time, Hector came rushing in, gun in hand, scanning the room for the source of the threat.

"What's wrong?!" Reggie asked with concern.

Samantha's breaths came in short bursts. Her trembling fingers clutched at her stomach as if expecting to find a wound there.

"I'm dead," she gasped, sitting back down on the couch.

"Calm down," Reggie said as she sat down beside her. "It was just a dream, okay?"

Hector, still by the door, watched as Samantha tried to pull herself together. Reggie turned to him with a reassuring nod. "It's okay. I've got her."

Hesitating, he lowered the gun, then gave a short nod before stepping back into the hall.

"It was just a silly nightmare," she said, smiling softly as she brushed the sweaty hair out of her sister's face. "You almost gave me a heart attack, you dick."

In the studio, with music playing softly from the speakers, Hector was back on the floor and resumed a set of rapid sit-ups. His movements were relentless as he pushed his body to the limit to block out the chaos unfolding in his head. It was all he could do. When he tried to sleep, he just saw that girl again, torn apart and eaten by the things on the street. He could cover his horror when he was awake, but while asleep, he had no protection from seeing that all over again.

After a few minutes, the studio door opened, and Reggie walked in. She paid no attention to his exercises and just walked over to a nearby chair and sat.

"How is she?" Hector asked, out of breath as he collapsed back to the floor.

"Okay, I guess," she sighed. "I left her to it. You don't mind if I hang with you?"

"Not at all," he said as he sat up. "But I gotta tell you something. I'm gonna head down to San Diego tomorrow."

Reggie frowned. "San Diego? What for?"

"My mom's down there. My sister. Her kids. Friends. I gotta check in on them."

"You know they . . . they might not be alive . . . right?" Reggie said quietly.

"Yeah, I know," Hector replied. "But I gotta know for sure, right?"

Reggie got off the chair and settled onto the floor beside him, stretching her legs out. "Are you all close?"

"Yeah. Pretty close, I guess." He chuckled. "A normal Puerto Rican family. Our love language is yelling and screaming at each other." He turned to her. "You? What about your family? Apart from your sister."

Reggie scoffed, shaking her head. "Nah. Just me and her. My mom was killed when I was young, when some guys broke into our house. My dad freaked after that."

"Ah, hence all the gun know-how?"

She nodded. "He made sure we could handle just about anything . . . He kind of stopped being our father and just became Colonel Belmont." She paused, looking sad. "Then he married Doris for some reason, and she just went about spending all the money she could. He's on the other side of the world, though . . . I have no idea if he saw the comet."

Hector studied her for a moment, feeling sorry. "What about that guy? The one you lost earlier?"

"Larry?" Reggie considered him, then let out a short breath. "I dunno. He could be alive somewhere. He made it past the comet. He could have run home. I was gonna break up with him anyway. I don't wanna be a dick, but I'm glad he's not here."

Hector smirked. "Dumped in the apocalypse? Harsh."

Reggie turned to him. "Should we come to San Diego with you?"

"You should both stay here in case that phone goes again. If Samantha was right and they wanted to save us. So, I'll come back, I promise. Even if my family is alive, I'll come back. And if these people come and pick you up, leave a note for me by the door."

In the executive office, Samantha lay on the couch in the dark, staring at the ceiling. She couldn't sleep. Not if it meant encountering that demonic cop again. Instead, she was just listening. The studio was only next door, and the walls were not that thick. Even with the music playing softly in the background, she could hear Reggie and Hector's voices.

"Are you worried about me?"

"Yeah," Reggie replied without hesitation.

A low chuckle followed. "Tell you what. Before I go tomorrow, we'll run down to that place and get us some real guns. That should make everybody feel safer. Okay?"

As she lay there, unable to do anything except eavesdrop, another thought pushed its way to the surface.

Her skin. It *tingled*.

She reached down and scratched absently at her arm.

Then again.

And again.

The city was as silent as it had been the day before, morning light cresting the same crimson hue.

With the La Brea Tar Pits behind them, Reggie turned and saw the large mammoths stuck in place, their fiberglass bodies streaked with dust and grime, and they looked as if they were drowning in the pits. Once a harmless attraction for tourists and school field trips, it now looked surreal on these empty streets. The way the red sky cast its hue over this prehistoric scene. It felt unreal. Like a cheap B-movie.

Reggie sadly exhaled. "Even the fake dinosaurs outlived everyone."

Her thoughts were suddenly shattered as a deafening burst of automatic gunfire erupted, filling the air with sharp cracks as bullets ripped through metal.

The late-model sedan, parked on the other side of the street, jerked violently under the sudden onslaught of lead. The glass shattered, the tires burst, and the chassis became riddled with holes as the rounds tore through it like paper.

Samantha stood at the center of it all, gripping an Uzi like she was born with it in her hands. Bullet casings ejected wildly, bouncing off the pavement as her finger held steady on the trigger. Her expression was hard and very focused. Every shot was a release, every burst dragging her upset and fear away.

Beside her, Reggie held a similar weapon, but she had no interest in firing it. Instead, forgetting the tar pits, she stood with her fingers jammed into her ears and a grimace etched on her face.

Soon, the sedan was obliterated, effectively killed, as Samantha let go of the trigger.

What was once a vehicle had turned into junk.

Reggie was the first to break the silence. She lowered her hands from her ears, shaking her head at the vehicular carnage. "Well, that car won't be bothering us anymore."

Samantha turned to her, still gripping the smoking gun, her expression steeled. "Tell me, d'you make it with him last night?"

Reggie blinked. "Make it? Who? Hector?"

Samantha scoffed, her eyes burning with accusation. "No, the Good Humor Man. Who d'ya think I'm talking about?"

Reggie sighed with exasperation. "Really? Is that what's bugging you this morning? You've been in a shit mood with me since you woke up."

"Just tell me."

"In all of this, with what's happening to us. All this bullshit, *that's* what's up your ass? Whether I hooked up with him?"

"That's not an answer, man!"

"No, I didn't make it with him last night." She said firmly. "Where the hell did this come from?"

Samantha let out a hollow laugh. "Oh, right, Reg. Why should I be weirded out? My sister, who's swiped every guy I've ever had my eye on, has now swiped the last guy in the whole damn world. Yeah, that's outta left field, ain't it?"

"Every guy? You mean the guys my age in my year that you decided you had some claim to?" She let out a sharp breath. "Yeah, I'm really sure that's reality, Samantha."

For a moment, they just looked at each other, tension sparking between them like a live wire. Then something shifted.

The absurdity of the argument, of where they were, of everything, suddenly hit them both at once.

At the end of the world, they were standing on an empty street with semi-automatic machine guns, arguing about boys who were probably all dead and which one would have the last boy alive.

It started small, just a smirk, a barely contained chuckle. And in the space of a breath, it unraveled completely. Laughter bubbled up, uncontrollable, ridiculous, growing, until they were both guffawing outright.

The weight of the world momentarily lifted.

But as quickly as it started, it faded again.

Reality settled back in.

The last echoes of laughter died on their lips.

Maybe it wasn't so funny after all.

The City of San Diego lay under the same red blanket that claimed Los Angeles. The skyline stood against the haze, silent and empty, the streets below showing no signs of life.

The sound of a diesel engine rumbled before Hector's truck came into view, driving through the residential streets of Rancho Peñasquitos. Each neighborhood here was the same as the last. The same as in L.A. Empty, with piles of clothes dotted across the streets, lawns, and sidewalks.

Hector had little emotional reaction to any of it. It all seemed too strange to be real. The idea that people had simply vanished, leaving behind nothing but empty garments and red dust? It was easier to believe they had been raptured right off the face of the Earth. It was the things he saw that disturbed him. The flesh-eating things. The piles of clothes were just that, and he could not connect them to the people who once wore them.

It wasn't until he saw a pile of clothes with a leash

trailing away from it that something inside him clicked. A leash that led to a small collar beside its own tiny mound of dust.

That was when he felt the weight of sadness about them.

The thought of people disappearing was impossible enough—but animals, too? He could picture the moment . . . the dog standing there, its owner holding the leash, maybe pulling slightly to keep it from darting ahead. Staring up at the comet's light in confusion. Then, in an instant . . . gone. No warning. No sound. No struggle. Just a collar and a leash where an innocent life used to be.

He soon pulled up in front of a small, well-kept house. In this neighborhood, some homes had been maintained with care, while others had fallen into neglect, their yards overgrown and their windows cracked. But Hector's house, his mother's house, stood neatly behind its chain-link fence, just as it always had.

Opening the door, he soon heard it.

A scratchy Latin song drifted out from inside, the lively, familiar tune filtering through the still air.

As he walked up the path, Hector suddenly felt a pang of hope. Maybe, *just maybe*, his mother had made it. Maybe she was inside, waiting.

A smile crept across his face. "Mamá, soy yo, estoy bien!" he called out as he picked up his pace and dashed toward the front door.

It only took a single moment after he stepped inside the house for all his hopes to be dashed.

The music was coming from an old, battered phonograph that was sitting on a shelf in the living room. Its record arm had been left up, and as the tone arm reached the end of the record, it raised, swung back, lowered, then began playing the same record from the start.

That joyful sound it played felt like a cruel joke as Hector looked up, thinking for a moment, taking in the enormity of what he was now having confirmed.

Next to the phonograph, he saw a framed picture on the shelf. His mother, smiling at him. And next to that were more small frames, each with different family members. His sister, his nephews. His uncles, aunts, grandparents. All looking happily out at him. None of whom knew then what he knew now.

He stared at them for a while before getting the nerve up.

He walked to the kitchen window.

He forced himself to see what was in the yard. The yard his family did everything in.

Piles of clothes.

His family.

His lip quivered.

Pull yourself together, Hector. You can't change what happened.

For the next twenty minutes, he sat alone at the kitchen table, crying.

With the tears drying on his cheeks, Hector forced himself to stand. He had one mission here. He would grab things from here and then head back to KJJR.

Rushing up to the bedrooms, he grabbed a pillow-case from the bed and walked from room to room, looking for any keepsakes he wanted as a reminder. A baseball cap, a high school yearbook, an old trophy, his mom's hairbrush, a handful of framed pictures, and his abuela's bible. He shoved each of them into the pillowcase and made his way back down to the kitchen.

From the fridge, he grabbed two bottles of his mother's homemade salsa. And as he turned, he saw something else . . . a small plastic box labeled *Recipes*.

He hesitated before opening it. He could almost hear his mother's voice, teaching him how to make her favorite dishes as they stood in front of the stove, using the cards in the box as guides.

He was about to smile in his memories but was interrupted.

A sound.

A low, rasping breath like a growl from outside. Barely audible over the music.

Cautiously, he hurried through to the living room and switched off the power to the phonograph, plunging the house into silence.

He reached for his gun, not the cheap Saturday Night Special he had back in Los Angeles but a real weapon, a .45 service revolver, that was tucked into the back of his jeans. Taken from the same weapons cache he had taken Reggie and Samantha to this morning.

That sound came again.

A slow, wet inhalation.

With a gun in one hand and a full pillowcase in the

other, he moved toward the front door. Pressing his ear up against the wood, he listened intently.

Then, after a moment, that sound was right outside the door.

"Hey," Hector called out. "I've got a gun, puta, and I'll use it."

No one replied, but the ragged breathing started to sound more feral. Hungrier.

Hector took a deep breath in and steadied himself. "Okay . . ." he said softly, hearing his pulse louder than his breathing.

Cocking the gun, he braced himself for what was to come. He slowly put the pillowcase down and unlocked the door as quietly as he could.

In one swift motion, he quickly flung the door open, ready for whatever monster was on the other side.

The front yard was empty.

For a split second, Hector's brow furrowed. He stood, confused . . .

. . . Until a movement below him caught his eye.

He peered down. It was a monster for sure, but it was also a child. Or at least something that used to be a child. This boy couldn't have been more than eight or nine, but his skin was pale and cracked like he was ancient. He stood there, diminutive. Staring up at Hector. Snarling with blank, milky eyes. The same horrible look that was on the things he saw eating the hitchhiker.

Instantly, Hector threw himself back into the house and slammed the front door shut behind him.

"Oh, hell no!" he shouted, gripping the gun.

The kid lunged at the closed door, thudding against the wood outside in an almighty, sudden rage.

Another loud *thud* came. This time, it shook the walls around the door. The picture of John F Kennedy his mother insisted on hanging in the hallway rattled and tilted under this attack.

"Get the fuck away from here, kid!" Hector shouted. "I don't want any of what you're sellin'!"

Another *thud*.

With the gun aimed at the door, Hector tried to figure out what in the hell he was supposed to do. He wasn't afraid, not really of a little kid, even a zombie one . . . but this was . . . insane. Was he allowed morally to shoot a kid if it was trying to kill him? If there was a priest he could ask, he would.

"I'm not kidding about the gun, kid!" he shouted. "I'll pop a hole in your face if you don't leave. *Now!*"

The fourth *thud* was the hardest yet, and as it sounded, the door split wide open. Breaking into two splintering pieces.

"Aw, come on!" Hector shouted in disbelief as he aimed the gun.

But the kid didn't hesitate against the weapon's threat. Instead, he just charged.

Feeling a sudden pang of nerves, Hector stumbled backward, into the living room, knocking over a chair, then another. His foot caught on the end table, sending a lamp crashing to the floor. He scrambled to his feet, dodging around furniture as the thing came after him, relentless.

I can't kill a kid . . . I just can't.

As he moved, his shoulder clipped against the phonograph, sending the needle down and the turntable spinning once more.

Suddenly, the house was filled with loud, blaring mariachi music. It was almost comical. The cheerful, upbeat tune played over the sound of furniture breaking as the kid snarled and roared in an animalistic rage.

"Mamabicho," Hector cursed under his breath.

Trying for a second time, he pointed the gun straight at the kid's head, but it was useless. He couldn't bring himself to pull the trigger. Sure, this was a monstrous flesh-eating thing, but the Scooby Doo T-shirt he wore was a reminder that whatever it was used to be a regular child.

"Goddammit," he seethed as he made a split-second decision. He grabbed the full pillowcase of keepsakes as he made a run for the door.

But the kid was fast. So fast that he quickly blocked the way out and forced Hector's escape back into the house.

Barely managing to slam himself into the bathroom and lock the door, Hector braced his weight upon it as the kid followed, throwing his weight against it with a growl.

"This is so dumb," Hector uttered. "Why am I running from a fucking little kid? Just shoot him, Hector. Shoot him in the fucking skull."

But he knew he couldn't.

A second later . . . *Crash!* A tiny, grasping hand

punched through the thin bathroom door, with fingers reaching downwards for the knob.

Hector's eyes went wide.

Without wasting another second, he turned. Shoving open the bathroom window, he climbed out, pulling the full pillowcase behind him.

The moment his feet hit the grass outside, Hector ran.

All he could think was that the kid knew about the doorknob. He knew enough in his little zombie brain about how to open doors. Which was more than an animal would know.

CHAPTER
FIVE

Reggie and Samantha were sitting on the curb across from the decimated sedan. The drowning mammoth model still sinking into the tar pits behind them.

With their machine guns resting at their feet, they sat back, watching the world go by, a world that had so thoroughly abandoned them.

The phone lines were dead. No calls were being made anywhere, and they didn't want to lock themselves inside the radio station. Instead, they would write down where they were every time they left KJJR so that, when Hector returned, he could find them. They probably should have been afraid of the pale monsters that lurked on these streets, but with the machine guns, they felt invulnerable. So, they locked the radio station doors, hid a key under a rock nearby, and ventured out, armed to the teeth.

Around them were snacks raided from the nearby 7/11. Drinks, sweets, jerky, packaged sandwiches. Anything they could want from the store.

"Where are those zombies, then?" Samantha asked, looking around the streets. "We've been making a racket and haven't seen one!"

"Maybe they disappeared, too?" Reggie replied, not knowing the answer.

With a shrug, Samantha tilted her head back and drained a can of 7UP, not bothering to wipe her mouth as she tossed the empty can into the gutter.

Reggie looked disapproving. "That's about the twelfth one you've had this morning."

"Thirsty work this surviving, I tell ya," Samantha retorted, cracking open another one.

"Yeah? And what happens when your complexion freaks out? All the dermatologists are dead, you know."

"True . . . and to make shit worse, I'm getting a rash and have no one I can see about it," she said as she scratched her arm.

"Yeah, you and your rashes," Reggie snorted. "Forever cursed to wander the wasteland, itching."

"Forever . . . Huh . . ." Samantha took a breath. "I'm gonna tell you something, Reg. But you *gotta* promise not to tell anyone."

The sheer stupidity of that statement made Reggie laugh, an actual, *real* laugh that didn't feel like it belonged in a world like this. "Okay, I'll make sure none of my friends know."

"I'm serious," Samantha pressed.

"Okay. Fine. I won't tell anyone . . . What is it?"

Samantha hesitated, rolling the can between her fingers. "I'm still a virgin."

Reggie's smirk disappeared. Of all the things that

had happened in the last day or so, this was the one that caught her completely off guard.

"What about . . . at camp? You said Derek—"

"Made it up." Samantha shrugged. "Made him up. Made it all up."

"Shit," Audrey said as she sat in the computer room of the facility. On screen the words *ACCELERATION* flashed at her.

Thinking for a second, she quickly jabbed a sequence of numbers into the keyboard in front of her.

ERROR: INCORRECT CODE, the message updated.

She stared at the screen for a second, then at the keyboard. "What's the damn code, Audrey?" she said to herself.

She tried another combination.

ERROR: INCORRECT CODE.

This was a code that she had known by heart for over a decade. The code that escaped her.

She tried another.

ERROR: INCORRECT CODE.

"Shit!"

Taking a breath, she grabbed a pen and turned to the open notepad on the desk.

Loss of Memmery, she slowly wrote.

For a second, she looked at what she had written and smirked at the irony. She slowly crossed out the word Memmery and slowly wrote beneath it.

M

E

M

She paused, deep in thought of the word, before continuing.

O

She paused again, confused. Slowly, she wrote the only letter she could think of to go next.

V

"We found those survivors," Carter announced as he appeared in the doorway, stealing her from her memory lapses. "How long did you say the blood tests should take?"

Audrey thought for a moment. "Not long at all. I could test them within twenty minutes of taking their blood."

"Good," he replied stoically. "Come with me."

Walking down the long corridor away from the computer room, Carter continued as Audrey walked beside him, looking unsure.

"I spoke to the others," he said, "and we all agree with your analysis. There is absolutely no point in bringing any potentially contaminated subjects back here. That is too much of a risk in case they've been exposed."

They rounded a corner and entered the open, waiting elevator.

He continued. "So, we decided that we would like you to go with the group into Los Angeles and test them there."

"Whatever the majority wants," Audrey said, resigned, unable to hide the tinge of disdain.

Once inside the elevator, Carter pushed the up button.

As the doors closed and they started to ascend, he spoke without even looking at her. "You do not seem to hold our majority rule in high regard. Do you?"

"If something's wrong, it's wrong," she replied, deadpanning. "Whatever the majority says about it does not alter that one undeniable fact. But I'll go. I'll tow the party line. I just don't think we have any right to do any of this."

"But it goes to the core purpose of our whole group . . . to survive. You joined us to do that very thing. That is why we are here. It's the *only* reason we are here. Whether it's survival of a nuclear war or survival of something unforeseen, like this comet."

"Exactly my point," Audrey replied. "The *purpose* of the group never included bringing outsiders to the facility. This is about *our* survival against the end. Not bringing others into it."

She was never one to suffer fools gladly or at all, and she saw herself high above the people she was stuck in here with. They were too emotional, whereas Audrey was all about cold, hard facts and unassailable logic.

Soon, the elevator doors opened, not inside the facility but into a small concrete building. A building of one room with a single metal door that led outside, into the desert . . . to where the red haze colored everything.

This whole complex sat in the middle of nowhere, a

cluster of blockhouses behind chain-link fences. A row of four-wheel-drive utility vehicles on one side. Storage buildings on the other. Beyond it, miles of empty desert stretched to the horizon, the heat warping the distance into wavering mirages.

From one of the small blockhouses, Audrey and Carter soon emerged, still in the middle of their tense conversation. It was obvious that neither of them liked each other, but they tolerated each other nonetheless.

Above, the sound of a helicopter chopped through the air, drowning out their conversation. The Huey, old but still functional, hovered above the facility before starting its descent, touching down in a swirl of dust and heat.

Audrey watched as it landed, and something in her steely expression shifted as she caught sight of the passengers disembarking.

Survivors.

Men and women, dazed but alive, stepped carefully from the chopper with the help of two of the facility's guards. Among them, two small figures clung to each other, a boy and a girl, no older than seven, both wide-eyed and silent.

Audrey looked visibly perturbed.

"Children?" she exclaimed to Carter. "Are you kidding me?"

Carter didn't respond. He just watched as the survivors were guided toward the entrance of the facil-ity, who were looking terrified.

•   •   •

The department store within the Beverly Center mall was alive with sound.

In the electronics section, dozens of stereos were blasting out the same rock song from their speakers, creating a deafening racket throughout the building, sending the beat pulsing down the empty aisles.

This was the kind of store that any teenager would dream of running amok in. And with the end of the world having made an appearance, Reggie and Samantha were living that very dream.

In the sporting goods section, Samantha wore a pair of roller skates, and they slid back and forth against the floor in time with the music as her hips swayed on the offbeat.

Her new outfit was perfect. Satin shorts, a loose T-shirt, the kind of thing she'd have worn to the mall even before everyone vanished.

She ran a brush through her hair, the tag still dangling off its handle, then turned to check herself out in one of the full-length mirrors.

She approved of what she saw.

Pushing off a counter, she tossed the hairbrush behind her. She rolled out of the sporting section and down the long aisle towards the jewelry displays. As she gained speed, she moved back and forth across the aisle, weaving through displays of handbags and coats.

From another aisle, a second skater soon joined her. One with a wide grin. Reggie. She was also in her element as she turned around and started skating backward, just as fast and just as in control.

Sidling up to a rack of fur coats, Samantha grabbed

one from a hanger and draped it over her shoulders. Immediately, she struck a dramatic pose, then tossed it aside.

Reggie, meanwhile, rolled around a display of sunglasses and grabbed a pair, putting them on and pirouetting on the wheels in a deft display before moving to the next section.

As the song ended and the next played, then the next, then the next, the two sisters had forgotten about life and just laughed and smiled. They raided accessories, jewelry, and anything that caught their eye. As they went from section to section, they had no cares. They just left a trail of discarded items in their path.

For a while, nothing outside the store existed as they twirled through the aisles, reveling in the absurdity of having an entire department store to themselves.

But they were not alone.

High above, a small black security camera watched them closely, its lens shifting as it zoomed in to get a closer look.

Oblivious to this surveillance, Samantha rolled up beside Reggie, holding two shirts on hangers.

"Which do you like better? Pink or yellow?"

Reggie pointed to the bright pink one. "Pink."

With a smile, Samantha dropped the yellow one to the floor, took the pink shirt off its hanger, and put it on over her T-shirt. "Me too."

In the dark surveillance office, the black-and-white monitors continued to zoom in on the girls as they went about their spree. There was no music in this room, only the hum of the air conditioning in addition to one other thing: low, asthmatic breathing.

Willy leaned toward the monitors, the screens' glow catching his wraparound sunglasses. He was young, barely out of his teens, with spiked hair and the kind of pallid complexion that never saw the sun. His expression remained blank as his head turned toward others who were with him in the room. Waiting patiently for his orders.

Three stock boys stood to the side, their clothes stained with the grime of the store's underbelly.

"Okay," Willy said with a smile, his voice low and rasping. "Let's fuckin' do this, then."

Without hesitation, the stock boys immediately moved in unison, filing out of the room.

Willy turned back to his monitors, keeping a nasty smile on his face as he oversaw what was about to happen.

Samantha wore her new pink shirt, complete with the price tag hanging loose from its sleeve.

Across the aisle, Reggie leaned over a display case, applying eye shadow in the mirrored countertop.

"I've been thinking," Samantha said, musing.

"Don't you go setting no dangerous precedents here," Reggie retorted with a laugh as she blended the color on her eyelid.

"What if Hector's got the same problem we have?"

Reggie looked at her. "Such as?"

"Such as no guys?"

"You lost me . . . What?"

"I mean, what if Hector's gay?"

Reggie, her mouth slightly open, considered it for half a second before shaking her head. "Yeah, no. That's not . . . That's not him."

Samantha smirked. "Think it over. You said he didn't come on to you last night, right?"

"So? He said he went with that girl during the comet."

"Let's forget that possible lie for one second, okay? Now, look at the facts. Fact one, most men—and it annoys me to say it—find you smokin' hot. Fact two, he may very well be the last man on Earth." She paused but didn't give Reggie time to say anything. "So, with those two facts, that means that the last guy on Earth is either a gentleman or gay. I mean, c'mon . . . We're in Los fucking Angeles. One of the gayest towns on Earth, and no one is a gentleman anymore!"

Reggie stopped what she was doing, turning to glare at her sister, and let out a slow, pointed *tsk*.

Samantha grinned. She may have been joking, but she was not suggesting anything out of the realm of possibility.

Reggie bent back down to the mirrored counter to finish her makeup.

"Attention, shoppers . . ." The department store's PA system crackled loudly to life.

Reggie's head shot up as Samantha froze.

• • •

In the surveillance room, Willy was talking into the microphone. His tone was thick with a cruel tinge. "I hope you have the money to pay for all of that stuff you've taken."

"Where's your weapon?" Reggie whispered as she backed up to her sister.

"In daytime casuals, with my cheer stuff."

Reggie winced. "Damn. I left mine in stereo." She grimaced, trying to think of a plan. "Shit. I'm glad Dad's not around to see this."

Samantha's voice was just above a whisper. "Rule number one . . ."

They spoke in unison.

"Ladies, cover your ass at all times."

Samantha moved first, skating silently across the main floor. She was fast, good on her feet, rolling backward every few moments to check her flank.

Reggie weaved through the aisles, keeping to the shadows, darting between mannequins and shelving units.

They were not just Valley girls. They were Valley girl commandos. Sure, their training came from the confines of their suburban house, but the colonel's regiment had been relentless, and now, they called upon each and every lesson.

And as they moved, the sounds of laughter echoed from multiple places within the store. Like hyenas, this laughter was unhinged and echoed over the music still playing from the electronics department.

It only took a minute for Samantha to silently reach the daytime casual section. But she was too late. She looked around. There, on the bench, was her cheerleader uniform, folded just as she left it, but there was no sign of her gun.

The PA crackled again.

"What's the matter? You lost something?" Willy said in a mocking tone. "You should check in Lost and Found. Up on the second. But I don't think it will be there."

In the electronics section, where the music was still blaring, Reggie spotted her Uzi shoved between a stack of car radios.

"You didn't find this one, asshole," she muttered, snatching it up and cocking it in one swift motion.

She moved fast, crouching behind an aisle, aware they were being watched. Looking up, she scanned the ceiling . . . and there it was. A closed-circuit camera, its motor humming as it swept the floor, searching.

Then a voice crackled over the PA, light and teasing. "Where'd you go, huh?"

Reggie didn't hesitate. She sprang up over the aisle, lifted her gun, and fired.

A volley of bullets split the air, shattering the camera in a burst of sparks and broken plastic.

Willy's reaction over the PA was one of uncontrolled fury. "Fucking whore! That was my camera!" he screamed. "Get her, men. Get her now."

From behind the counters on the other side of the room, two stock boys sprang up, opening fire. One held Samantha's missing Uzi, while the other carried two handguns. They fired in Reggie's direction without any hesitation.

Caught by surprise, Reggie skated backward away from the gunfire at too fast a speed. She quickly lost her balance and crashed hard onto the floor as her feet flew out in front of her.

"Shit," she gasped painfully as another volley of gunfire headed her way and flew over the aisle and into the shelves nearby. She closed her eyes and stayed down in a huddle.

Just from these few moments, she could tell one thing. These boys may have guns, but their aims sucked. She also knew that they did not have unlimited ammunition.

Across the store, Samantha had ducked behind a counter. As the gunfire stopped, she did not want to do what she was about to do, but she had to let her sister know where she was.

"Reg?" she called out in the quelled silence.

The stock boys hesitated, guns turning to where her voice was coming from.

"Let's get her instead," one whispered to the other. "She's got no gun."

They crept forward, guns raised, weaving between the displays, closing in on the sound of Samantha's voice.

A stupid move.

From behind them, Reggie shot out from behind another aisle, skates gliding, Uzi raised.

She opened fire.

The stock boys dropped for cover as bullets ripped through the shelves around them.

They quickly regrouped and fired back.

Glass shattered, mannequins collapsing, and televisions exploding.

The store had erupted into a veritable war zone.

Reggie pressed herself low as bullets cut into the shelves above her.

She waited as bullet after bullet whizzed by. Waiting for them to reload. Eventually, when the gunfire stopped and the silence filled the floor again, she shouted out.

"Look, we're expecting friends here at any minute. You guys better split while you got a chance!"

After a short silence, the hyena-like laughter erupted again, and the stock boys resumed firing.

Reggie curled up, covering her head again. Her bluff had failed miserably.

The helicopter cut through the haze above the husk of what had once been L.A., its rotor blades shattering the silence below. Nearing the Arco Towers, it banked hard, sweeping around the glass monoliths in a tight arc before angling toward downtown.

A barrage of music played out loudly from the electronics department of the store.

Low down, between the aisles in housewares,

Samantha had ditched her skates and was walking barefoot. She crept silently; each step carefully placed as she made her way toward Sporting Goods.

The sign above the aisle confirmed her direction. *Ahead in Sporting Goods: All rifles, 20% off.*

From elsewhere in the store, the manic laughter echoed. The stock boys were busy pinning Reggie down, taunting her from their position, finding it all very amusing. But they were so invested in her that they hadn't noticed Samantha slip along the wall and past them.

As she crept, she paused and glanced over her shoulder to make sure no one had followed. She was resolute in her plan. She *needed* a weapon to help her sister, and Sporting Goods was where she had to get one.

With her rear clear, she smiled, turned back to keep on, and immediately stopped cold.

Less than a foot away, grinning ear to ear, stood the third stock boy. A knife clasped in his hand, he held up to her.

She gasped in fear but only for a second. Almost instantly, she forced herself to regain control, tilting her head up to the boy with a perfectly innocent, girlish smile.

"Why, hello there," she said with a sudden flirtatiousness.

His smile faltered as he was caught off guard. His knife lowered slightly.

Samantha then drove her knee straight up into his

groin. Hard. Very hard. Twice. And both were perfectly aimed.

A choked scream burst from the stock boy's mouth as he doubled over, dropping his knife. Before he had a chance to react, she pivoted and delivered a swift, brutal boot to his face, knocking him out cold.

Samantha didn't wait around to admire her handiwork.

As she ran across the aisle, the other stock boys heard their friends cry and walked over. Leaving Reggie.

Seeing Samantha, they turned their gunfire her way. Bullets flew around her, shattering glass as she sprinted across the open floor, zigzagging.

From her position, Reggie stood and opened fire, catching the stock boys off guard as they were focused on her sister.

Quickly, they turned their aims back to her.

Huddled behind a rack of pots and pans, Samantha tried to catch her breath. But as the bullets stopped firing her way, she did not have time to move. A blur came from behind her, knocking her to the floor. Within seconds, a heavy knee slammed down on the back of her neck.

As her face was being pressed into the stone tile, something cold and metallic pressed against the back of her head. The barrel of a .38 Magnum.

Above her, Willy grinned, exposing a jagged row of yellowed enamel.

"You made me leave my base," he said. "Now you gotta make it worth my while." He then raised his voice. "I got your friend," he called in Reggie's direction. "You better give yourself up, or *else*!"

The two stock boys walked over to where Reggie had been. Guns up at the ready. But she was no longer there. The aisle was empty.

"You hear me?" Willy called out again. "I have her. Now, give up! The game's over. You lost. We won." He quickly got more annoyed. "You better get your ass out here *now* or just see what I'll do to her pretty face. I'll rip it right off!"

Still, no response.

"You ever see a skeleton scream?"

The stock boys had searched all the aisles in the area but had come up empty-handed.

Then, slicing through the air, came a *hiss* of polyurethane wheels rolling on the store floor.

The sound of Reggie's roller skates.

The polished chrome on her boots glinted under the flickering store lights as she skated forward, slow and deliberate.

She wasn't alone.

Walking in front of her, his posture stiff, was the third stock boy . . . her prisoner. He stumbled, not only unnerved by the Uzi she trained on his back but the sore groin he still had from Samantha's attack. Her two attacks.

Hearing her approach, Willy turned. He looked

extremely unimpressed at Reggie. With his gun still pointing at Samantha's head, he stooped and grabbed her by the neck, yanking her to her feet. She gagged as he gripped tight.

"Seems we have each other's property," Willy said with malicious glee to Reggie.

Her voice, on the other hand, came out emotionless and to the point. "Let her go, or I off your guy right now."

Willy studied her for a moment, considering. Then, almost lazily, turned the gun from Samantha and pointed it directly at them.

Stock boy number three stiffened, sweat breaking out across his pale forehead. His voice came out in a strained stutter. "C'mon, W-Willy, man. She m-means it."

Willy tilted his head slightly, regarding the stock boy with something between amusement and disappointment.

With a smirk, he then pulled the trigger.

The shot tore through the stock boy's sternum, blasting a fist-sized hole through his back in a spray of red mist, shattered bone, and ruined organs . . . just barely missing Reggie. The force of the bullet sent him hurtling backward, slamming into her, and drenching her in blood as they crashed to the floor. He landed with a wet, meaty slap. She hit with a pained thud.

Instantly, she scrambled to get to her feet, slipping on his blood as she fought to keep her balance. "You're crazy!"

Willy smirked, moving his grip from Samantha's

neck to her hair. Winding his finger around the strands to keep her from squirming.

"Oh, I'm not crazy," he said casually. "I just don't give a fuck."

The car that had been used as target practice opposite the tar pits stood, riddled with bullet holes. Glass and metal lay in small pieces across the asphalt beneath it and wisps of smoke billowed up from its cracked radiator.

A hundred yards away, the helicopter had settled down on an empty part of the street. From within, a few members of the desert facility stepped out. Oscar, Wilson, Audrey, and two guards. They were examining the scene they had noticed from the sky.

Oscar was at the still-smoking car and began to survey the wreckage. With his boot, he nudged a collection of spent shell casings on the ground. As he did, he nodded in that very official, detective-y way he imagined people did when they were piecing together clues. But in reality, he didn't have much idea what really happened.

"They were here," he said with the kind of gravitas that suggested he had cracked the case wide open. "I'm sure of it."

Next to him, Wilson walked up with his arms crossed. In his mind, he was already five steps ahead in the deductive reasoning game. "I still maintain that they wouldn't have wandered far," he said, looking at the empty streets around them. "Not with that much firepower."

Audrey cut in, sighing. Knowing that they didn't have much to go on. "Of course it was them. The note at the radio station said they were gonna be in this area. But, even so, we can't just search the whole city. We've got no other leads to go on. We don't know where they went."

Wilson scoffed. "Or and hear me out on this one. We apply some actual deductive reasoning."

Oscar, feeling like he was about to say something brilliant, nodded eagerly. "Yes! Let's think logically. Where would aimless adolescents go from here?"

They each looked around them and then realization hit them simultaneously.

The answer presented itself in the form of a towering billboard on the nearby building.

Dinosaurs Had Tar Pits.

You Have The Mall . . .

Come to the Beverly Center and shop in style.

Only 10 minutes away.

The mall—because, *of course,* kids went to the mall.

CHAPTER
SIX

DEEP in the Beverly Center's loading dock, the air reeked of cardboard and motor oil. The ventilation system for the whole building was down here, and it sounded like a jet engine as it pumped air around the mall. It was so loud that no one here had heard the helicopter, settling down in the parking lot outside.

Not that knowing that would have helped Samantha or Reggie's current plight.

They were bound back-to-back with packing tape, perched uncomfortably on a stack of wooden pallets. The tape dug into their arms, making their shoulders sore from the awkward position they were held in. Reggie shifted, testing the strength of the tape as she tried to find a weakness, but it was too thick and too tight.

They were caught in the stock boys' domain, surrounded in a loose circle by them and Willy. Their expressions ranged from amused to outright delighted.

This was their slice of fun for the day. A break from the usual monotony of night shifts at the mall. And since the comet had changed the city, it was a welcome source of new entertainment . . . one with no rules. None but Willy's.

He was the ringmaster, and this was his show. He paced, adjusting his sunglasses, smirking as his gang watched their prisoners.

"See, we busted our asses in this place," he announced. "All night, every night. Lugging your TVs, your fancy jeans, your overpriced sneakers. And you know what we got for it?"

He turned to Reggie and Samantha, waiting for an answer that wouldn't come.

"*Nothing*," he spat. "But we did it. Because we believed in the system. Thought if we worked hard enough, we'd move up. But guess what? The system's dead. And now? *We* make the rules. This is *our* mall. *Our* world."

In one sudden, dramatic movement, he crouched close to Reggie, so close she could feel his rotten breath against her cheek.

His voice dropped to a whisper. "Two days ago, we were stacking shelves." He grinned, getting even closer. "Now it's ours. That's the goddamn flag-waving, barbe-cue-eating, red, white, and blue, bald-eagle-my-coun-try-tis-of-thee American *fuckin'* way." He let his words hang in the air as his smile grew even wider. "And then you two show up. You show up and interrupt us. And we are so happy that you're here. We needed something to keep us entertained."

Reggie suppressed her panic, realizing the danger they were in. "What do you want?"

Willy's eyes never left hers. "I want to punish you for all the things you stole. *That's* what I want."

Samantha, beside her, huffed impatiently. "You want us to pay for that stuff? And for what? Ain't you all seen the worlds gone to shit?"

The stock boys snickered.

Willy stood, turning his attention to her and moved in close, crouching, their noses almost touching. It was her turn to smell his rancid breath. She turned her head away, trying to hold her own.

"I'll tell you a secret, okay?" he murmured. "You won't *believe* what I am going to do to you." He tilted his head, regarding her. "Not even in your worst nightmare would you have any idea . . ."

He grasped her chin, forcing her to look at him. Then, slowly, he removed his sunglasses. His milky eyes stared wide at her.

Reggie, looking at him over her shoulder, suddenly felt a wave of nausea. Realizing that he was the same as the man from the alley at the El Rey. The same as the people who ate Hector's hitchhiker.

Willy's grin remained. "Hey, I have an idea . . . you wanna play a game?" he asked, almost gently. "It's called Scary Noises."

Somewhere above them, in another part of the mall, Oscar and Audrey, rifles in hand, waited in the main concourse of the building.

Ahead of them, they watched Wilson come out of the department store shaking his head. "Somebody shot up the whole place," he said in hushed tones.

"How long ago?" Oscar said.

"You can still smell the smoke in there, so not long at all."

"Was it them?" Audrey asked.

Oscar shook his head. "Does it matter?"

"Close your eyes," Willy ordered.

Still bound on the palettes, they leaned their heads together, tightly shutting their eyes and clenching their teeth. Not knowing what was to come but expecting the worst.

A sharp loud metallic click then sounded from beside them.

"Isn't that a scary, scary noise?" Willy said, walking around, speaking in a light and teasing tone. "Wanna hear it again?"

Another sharp loud click.

Reggie forced herself to breathe evenly, to stop herself from panicking. She wasn't going to give this bastard the satisfaction.

Samantha, even without being told to, was doing the same. And neither of them needed to see what was happening to know that sound. That was the sound of a gun.

"Gosh," he said, mockingly thoughtful. "The suspense is killing me . . . and I guess it could kill you, too."

The click had indeed come from a gun. From Willy's .38 Magnum. One that he had pointed directly at Reggie's forehead.

"Let's play another round," Willy said.

He then pulled the firing pin back and pulled the trigger once more. For the third time, the metal click sounded as the pin hit the empty chamber.

He was playing Russian roulette with them as the targets.

"Now, wait a minute," Willy murmured, almost to himself. "I don't think there's actually a bullet in here."

The stock boys giggled, having a very hard time controlling their delight at what their leader was doing.

Cracking the barrel open, Willy turned the revolver in his hand like he was inspecting a delicate piece of machinery. He tilted it toward the light, and his face lit up.

"Oh," he crooned. "There it is." He snapped the chamber closed with a flick of his wrist. "See? I just needed to be patient. I'd get to it *eventually*."

He lifted the gun again and resumed aiming at Reggie's forehead.

"This is it, girls," he whispered. "I really think it is . . . So, let's end scary, scary noises . . . And now . . . we just end you both, okay?" He paused as he looked at them. "Hey, if I aim this right, I think one shot could go through *both* of your heads. Now, that's being economical with the ammunition, right? I mean, we *are* in a war, aren't we? We need to ration the bullets as best we can. Especially after today . . . So, that will be the game. I'll see if I can kill you both with the same bullet . . . and if I can, you both will go on a date with me. And trust me, neither of you want to be alive for that."

The next few moments went by slowly.

Reggie could feel the gun against her skin. She could hear the relentless pounding of her own heart. The sting of panic was coursing through her veins.

Samantha breathed as evenly as she could. She refused to accept this was happening. It couldn't be the end. It just *couldn't*. Maybe she could bargain with this asshole. Maybe—

But before she could speak, a deafening shot rang out.

The stock boys jumped.

Reggie flinched, but . . . she wasn't the one who had been shot nor had Samantha, who exhaled and laughed nervously.

They slowly opened their eyes.

Willy stood there, swaying, looking around in confusion.

A hole, small and precise, had appeared in the center of his forehead. Like a puppet cut from its strings, he then crumpled in a heap.

The loading dock doors then burst open as gunfire cracked through the stale air.

The expedition from the desert facility came in with guns blazing. Wilson, Oscar, Audrey, and the guards.

The stock boys tried to scramble, but they weren't fast enough.

Shots flew around the dock in a terrifying wave.

By the time they stopped, only Samantha, Reggie,

and those from the facility were left breathing. The two stock boys were lying in pools of their own blood near the loading bay exit.

Wilson stepped forward, surveying the scene, making sure they both were dead.

"I think they were infected, too," he said to Audrey. "Their lips. Cracked to all hell."

Audrey, meanwhile, looked at Willy's lifeless body, his milky eyes staring up at her.

She shivered.

An hour later, Reggie and Samantha leaned casually against the hood of a car in the parking lot of the Beverly Center. The sun was starting to go down behind the haze, making the crimson coloring of the city that much more vibrant.

Both were sipping from soda cans as they recounted their little adventure to one of the desert facility men, who listened politely. Their voices rose and fell with laughter, exaggerated gestures punctuating every wild detail.

Reggie mimed swinging a wooden plank at an invisible attacker. "And then . . . bam! Right in the face. I mean, I didn't want to, but the guy was built like a linebacker with the skin tone of a Wite-Out bottle, so . . . I did what I had to do."

Samantha took another long glug from her drink before scratching at her arm absently. Her skin still felt . . . off. Not itchy, exactly. Just sensitive. She didn't give it much thought. Not with everything else going on.

Across the lot, near the helicopter, Oscar and Wilson watched the girls from a distance. They were waiting for Audrey to finish the tests inside the chopper.

From inside, Audrey stepped out, two sheets of paper in her hands, having just tested their blood with her mobile scanner and noted down the results.

"I don't need to see the test results on the younger one," Oscar said. "I can guess . . . She has the itch already."

For a second, Audrey said nothing.

"Yeah, there's no use taking her back," she said finally.

Wilson shook his head. "This is going to be awkward. I expect they won't react well to being separated."

"I'll take care of her," Audrey said, her voice void of emotion. "And I can wait for this Hector to show up, test him, too."

Oscar and Wilson exchanged glances. The sudden shift in Audrey's attitude wasn't lost on either of them. She wasn't arguing but being cooperative. A trait she had not displayed in their years of knowing her.

"It's getting late," Oscar said, checking his watch. "We can't come back and get you tonight."

Audrey had other plans. "It's fine. I can drive. This city's full of cars. I don't need you to get me."

Wilson started to object, but before he could, Oscar cut in. "This sounds like a viable option." He hesitated.

"Of course, it's out of the question to let you remain here by yourself."

Audrey didn't react right away. Instead, she just stayed silent. Whatever she had planned, it clearly wasn't working out the way she had hoped.

"So, I'll stay with you," Oscar said, deciding for them. "But the older one? Let me see her results."

Audrey had no time to think of an excuse and handed over one of the pages.

Oscar looked at the figures and smiled. "Bingo. We have ourselves a contender!"

A few moments later, the helicopter lifted off, dust and debris swirling around the parking lot as it climbed higher into the darkening sky.

Samantha shaded her eyes, watching it disappear beyond the horizon, carrying Reggie along with it.

The department store had become a strange kind of sanctuary. After being the stronghold of the vicious Willy and the stock boys, it was a place of refuge for Samantha and Audrey as they walked through the bedroom department.

Audrey carried her black doctor's bag in one hand.

Samantha, meanwhile, sipped from yet another can of soda.

"So, listen," Samantha said, smacking her lips as she finished her sip. "Thanks for letting me hang here with you guys while I wait for Hector to come back."

"He knows to come back to the radio station?" Audrey asked.

Samantha nodded. "Yeah, we didn't have time to tell him we came here, but he will one hundred percent go there . . . So, we really should leave soon." Her gaze drifted across the showroom, where she caught sight of Oscar a few aisles away. He wasn't exactly hovering, but he was keeping an eye on what was happening—or, more specifically, on Audrey.

"Doesn't he like you?" Samantha asked.

"Look, I need you to lie down, okay?" Audrey said.

"What? Why?" Samantha replied.

Audrey gestured toward a nearby bed, a showroom display decked out in tacky floral comforters and perfectly arranged throw pillows.

Though at first hesitant, Samantha didn't have the energy to fight, so she got down onto the mattress, then placed the soda on the bedside stand. "What's this about, anyway? More blood samples? For what? What are you looking for?"

Audrey kneeled beside her, setting the doctor's bag on the edge of the bed and flipping it open. "Has your skin been dry? Irritated? I noticed you scratching your arm a lot."

"Yeah, I got a rash."

She absentmindedly scratched at her arm again, only realizing what she was doing when Audrey pulled a syringe from the bag.

Checking the needle with quiet efficiency, Audrey carried on. "The itching . . . It's one of the major symptoms of what has happened to everyone. Do you know that?"

Samantha stared at her, alarm flashing in her eyes. "Symptoms of the comet?" She let out a nervous laugh. "No, see . . . I *always* get rashes. This isn't anything to do with the comet. Like, if I have a fight with Doris or something, wham, bam, thank you ma'am, another rash appears. It's nerves. I mean, considering the last couple of days, I'm surprised I don't look like a giant piece of strawberry Jell-O."

She laughed at her own joke, but it was forced. A second later, she scratched her arm again, then immediately stopped, looking down at her hand as if it had just betrayed her.

Audrey's expression didn't change as she looked at Samantha and then over at Oscar.

He was still a few aisles away. Still watching.

Turning back, Audrey reached down into her bag. Her fingers ran over the tops of a set of tiny bottles inside until she found the one she needed.

"I'm going to give you something to help," she said.

Samantha looked wary. "And that'll take care of it?" She nodded toward the syringe. "I mean, if I *really* am . . . If it's not just a normal rash?"

"Sure will," Audrey replied.

Samantha let out a relieved breath. "God, you had me worried for a second."

Audrey smiled as she put the needle into the bottle and withdrew some of its liquid.

"Little pinch," she murmured.

Samantha barely had time to react before the needle slid under her skin of her arm.

"Ahhhh," she gasped. "Hey, who *are* you guys, anyway? Why are you even saving us?"

Audrey pulled the syringe back. "Oh, we're a sort of club," she said. "A think tank."

"So, you're, like, geniuses or something?"

Audrey smirked. "I thought we were, yeah."

"We've got a couple of geniuses at my school," Samantha snorted. "Both wimps."

Samantha barely got another word out before her eyelids fluttered. Her mouth sagged slightly open, her head lolling back against the pillow.

Audrey let out a breath she hadn't realized she'd been holding. She reached forward and gently brushed a strand of hair from Samantha's face.

"I'm sorry," she said.

She then started to feel a burning sensation in her fingers. A sudden intense itching.

No. Not now . . . Please . . . I need more time.

"Is that it?" Oscar said as he slowly approached. "She is neutralized? Did you give her enough?"

Without looking back, Audrey answered, "What did you want me to do, Oscar?" she asked sharply. "Take her out back and shoot her in the head?"

Oscar stepped nearer. "I simply was making sure," he said. "It's good it was painless. We're not monsters, after all."

Audrey didn't reply. Instead, she took a deep breath. Relaxing the tension from her face.

"We should go get a car and drive back now."

"But what about Hector?" he asked. "We could do with a second."

"We . . . I . . ." Audrey struggled to come up with a convincing reason. "We can't."

"Why on Earth not?"

She had no answer. No answer he would accept.

Oscar looked at her sternly. "What are you doing?" he said, his tone matching his expression. "What is this?"

Audrey's metaphorical back was against the wall.

"You better answer me," he ordered.

She turned, and he was standing a few feet away. She noticed his hand resting on the hilt of his wait-holstered gun. Ready to draw.

She smiled. "What are you going to do, Oscar? Shoot me?"

He persisted. "What are you not telling me, Audrey?"

His hand slowly gripped his gun.

She had no time. She had no option. She had to act.

Oscar motioned to the store around them. "This life is over. You get that, don't you? This is now survival of the fittest. It's—"

BANG.

The gunshot echoed around the bedroom depart-ment as Oscar stumbled in surprise.

His eyes were wide.

His breath gasping.

His heart bleeding.

In a slow, almost graceful motion, he fell to the floor.

He had not known that she had brought a snub-nosed pistol in her doctor's bag. Nor had he seen her grab it and aim at him.

Still holding the gun, Audrey's hands were shaking. Her breathing was fast and shallow.

Her eyes were starting to ache unnaturally.

Not yet.

She watched as Oscar breathed his last breath, with a look of bewilderment and pain.

Audrey's anguish then started to subside, as deep within her, she began to feel a rage. A brutal rage.

The city had not changed since the comet flew high above its skyline. This new order of things would remain. This was how the world was now. An empty, ghostly place, with only the rarest movement on its streets. A dry leaf skittered across the sidewalk. A shop sign swayed in the searching breeze.

The only noise here came from the weather. When the wind blew, it brushed against creaky gates or whistled through open windows.

But then . . . music.

Faint at first, just a distant tinge within the quiet. A song drifted closer between the glass buildings of downtown.

As the music grew louder, the city came to life in the reflection of a brand-new 1964 Chevy Impala Super Sport, freshly stolen from a San Diego dealership. It cruised across Redondo Junction and into the Fashion District. Low, sleek, and cherry, this car was a rolling dream—polished to perfection, the kind of vehicle that made people stop and stare.

If there were any people left to stop and stare.

Inside, Hector had one hand on the wheel, the other tapping lazily against the window frame to the beat of the music playing loudly from the tape player. The leather seats were so deep that only his head was visible above the window. He bobbed along with the music, fully in his own world.

Off East 4th Street, the Impala rolled up to the curb in front of the KJJR radio station, its tires crunching over a discarded newspaper as it came to a stop. The engine purred for a moment before Hector shut it off. He reveled in its sound.

Life may have turned into a nightmare, but at least he had little pleasures to escort him through it.

Swinging the door open, he stepped out, stretching like he had all the time in the world. And why not? He was feeling good. Sharp. He was not the same man who left here the day before. He had gone "shopping," just as Reggie and Samantha had and was dressed to the nines.

He looked either way up the street, making sure no white-eyed maniacs were stumbling nearby.

Wearing a crisp white disco suit, fresh out of *Saturday Night Fever*, he leaned into the back seat and pulled out his grand offering: two dozen long-stemmed red roses. He also grabbed a Fender electric guitar from the passenger seat, slung it over his shoulder, then adjusted his collar.

He was feeling smooth.

He climbed the steps to the station, walked over to the brick by the door and lifted it, expecting to find the key Reggie had put there. But it was gone.

His worry was short-lived as he looked up and saw that the key wasn't missing. It had been left in the door.

He shook his head in amusement.

"Keeping the place locked down, eh?" he mused.

Walking inside, he called out. "Hey, Regina! Samantha!" His voice echoed through the empty lobby. "Man, you gotta check out my ride. It's a '64 Impala, cleaner than a Jack in the Box taco!"

Through to the studio corridor, his pace slowed slightly, his excitement dimming a fraction . . . as he realized that something wasn't right. The music was no longer playing through the speakers. They had said they would keep it playing.

Maybe they had been saved by the voice on the phone? Maybe they turned it off before leaving?

The studio was dim. On his way here, he had expected the lights to be on and the girls to be playing loud music. In his mind, when he walked in, Samantha would be bouncing around, cracking jokes as Reggie rolled her eyes at how ridiculous his outfit was.

But there was none of that.

Just one figure.

Sitting on the floor in the corner of the room, staring back at him.

Hector stopped by the door as he saw her. Keeping her distance.

It was Audrey. Not that he had any idea who she was. She was wearing sunglasses, despite being in a darkened room. Her open medical bag was neatly at her side.

The gun in her hand, however, was anything but put aside. It was pointed directly at Hector.

For a time, neither of them spoke. Then, slowly, Audrey leaned forward. "My guess is that you're the legendary Hector Gomez?" she asked, her voice light and her tone casual. "I was just about to give up on you, you know . . . You took your sweet time."

Hector didn't reply. His hands were still full of roses and the guitar. He felt ridiculous. Like he'd just walked on to the wrong set in the middle of someone else's movie.

He glanced around the rest of the room.

There was no sign of the girls anywhere.

". . . Who are you?" he finally asked.

"*Every*body thinks I'm the villain, you know?" she said. "Even the actual villains think that."

Hector's gaze returned to the gun in her hand. "Well," he said, slowly, "I wonder why in God's green hell they'd they think that? Good guys always point guns at strangers, don't they?"

"No. Not that." Audrey's lips twitched uncontrollably. "It's because I didn't want to come in and get you people. *Any* survivors." Her voice was struggling to remain calm. "I mean, when I realized they weren't talking hypothetically anymore . . . Hell, it was my idea to use the transfusions as a way to quell an infection from those partially exposed. Those who saw that thing head-on were vaporized in a second. Those who only saw a reflection or were still outside became infected . . .

You all, you were lucky. You were hidden from the glow . . . But this . . . *this* was all just a survival scenario I came up with on the fly . . . I didn't think . . ."

She sighed and let the gun lower slightly, like she was already losing energy.

Hector didn't take his eyes off her.

She leaned back, her head resting against the wall, her fingers relaxing against the gun's grip. "That's what we did. Talk. Hypotheticals. What if the ice caps melted? What if India developed a viable delivery system for a nuclear device? What if the comet's photochemical theory was true?" She let out a soft, humorless laugh. "What if we took shelter in the facility? Would we survive? How would we ensure we did if . . . if . . ." She stared at the gun in her hand. "We were a little off on that one, by about five . . . maybe seven percent." A faint smirk as she turned the gun and offered it up to him. "You need this?"

"Nah," he said wearily. "I got one already."

Audrey's smile widened just slightly like she had expected that answer.

She flicked her hand toward the control panel to the right of him. "I left you a little something on there."

He didn't dare turn away from her in case it was a trap.

She then set the gun down beside her and pulled a syringe from her medical bag. Taking a small bottle, she filled the needle, flicking it to release any air bubbles, staring at it as she continued to talk.

"Anyway," she murmured, "I *thought* it was all hypothetical. Then they found those survivors."

She barely looked at him as she continued. "I told them . . . even if you terminate brain function, even if you keep them on straight oxygen and Hypernol . . . they just aren't going to produce enough blood . . . I had no idea how far they would go."

"What blood? Who?" Hector asked, dreading whatever answer she would say, not that he understood.

Audrey's expression didn't change.

"Damned desperate people do damn desperate things," she said simply. "And they were both desperate and damned."

Without any pause, she stabbed the needle into her own arm.

Hector could not do a thing before she pushed the plunger down.

She then let out a long, shaky, somewhat relieved breath as her eyes fluttered. But that didn't stop her lecture.

"And *then* there's the ethics," she continued, the words slowly starting to slur as her body began to list to one side. "But what are ethetehh . . ." She squeezed her eyes hard. Trying to focus. "What are *ethics* . . . ETH-ICS . . . to people . . . those who think they're better than everyone else?" She laughed softly, a bitter sound. "They're not *better*. They're just a bunch of assholes."

"Who are you talking about? Who are you? What survivors? What have you done with Reggie and—"

But she wasn't listening. She slumped back against the wall.

The gun slipped from her fingers.

Her breathing slowed.

And then, dead.

Hector stood, unsure of what he walked into. The roses in his hand felt heavier than ever.

Turning to the control panel, he noticed the yellow pad resting on there. Putting down the roses, he picked it up and began to read the pages and pages of scrawls.

As he got to the end of the second page, his eyes widened.

"Samantha . . ." he whispered.

CHAPTER
SEVEN

THE ROOM WAS WHITE. Not the warm soft white of china but the kind of white that hurt the eyes to look at. A too-clean, too-bright, too-sterile kind of white. A-hospital kind of white, illuminated by pale fluorescent strip lights.

Reggie didn't like this place. The moment she saw those concrete blockhouses in the middle of nowhere, she knew they'd be taking her underground. And if there was one thing she hated, it was that.

Bunkers. Basements and, yes, underground labs. They all had the same thing in common, like tombs with no easy way to escape. And Reggie did not do well in places where she felt trapped.

Her distrustful instincts had kicked in the second they led her through the heavy steel doors, down the elevator, and through the narrow corridors, beyond the multiple layers of security.

She memorized every corridor, every turn . . . just in case she had to bolt. But now, stuck at this metal table under harsh lights, with some lab coat creep grilling her about medical history, all she could think about was Samantha.

The man sitting across from her at the large ten-person table, was stone-faced and impassive, holding a large notepad and pen.

Carter. That's his name, she thought. He hadn't introduced himself, but Reggie had overheard it from one of the guards who left her in here. Not that names really mattered anymore. All that mattered was getting out and finding Samantha.

Without much of a preamble, he asked, "Have you ever had hepatitis?"

"Wow. No small talk? No 'Hey, how are you? How was your morning?' Just straight to *'Hey, Reggie, you got the hep?'*"

Carter didn't look up. Didn't even acknowledge her sarcasm. Just tapped his pen against the paper. "Please answer the question."

"No. I haven't."

"Diabetes?"

"Why do you care? What the hell kind of place is this?"

Carter, apparently immune to the conversation, just repeated himself. "Do you have diabetes?"

Reggie exhaled sharply. *"No."*

From the open doorway behind him, there was movement. She lifted her head slightly, catching sight of two kids just beyond the door, peeking in.

They were young. Maybe six or seven. Dressed in white hospital gowns, their feet bare against the cold tile. Their hair was still damp, as if they'd just been scrubbed clean.

Reggie offered them a small smile, but before either kid could react, two guards appeared behind them, ushering them away.

"Cute kids," Reggie said. "They part of this?"

"Survivors like yourself," Carter replied with disinterest as he cleared his throat, then carried on. "Anemia?"

She looked back at him, her patience thinning. "You gonna tell me what's going on? Or are we just gonna go down the list of fun diseases?"

He did not answer. He just kept his eyes on her.

"I had mono once. How's that? Caught it from the field backer Randy Sharp. Real piece of shit, that one . . . Now, tell me what's going on! Is this a weird underground hospital or something?"

"You are quite strong-willed, aren't you?"

"Cancer."

That word stole his attention in surprise. "You have cancer?"

Reggie smirked. "No. I *am* a Cancer. The star sign? I'm a homebody, and right now, I just want to know where the fuck I am, why the fuck I'm here, who the fuck you are, where the fuck my sister is—"

"Do you have anemia?" Carter asked pointedly.

Reggie glared in annoyance, enough that Carter knew he could not bully her into answering easily.

"This is a survival facility," he said, exhaling. "Built in 1978, privately funded. Designed to house up to twenty people along with a small security force. It was built through a private endowment to allow certain gifted people to survive in the event of a nuclear event."

Reggie, slowly, peered around the room.

Nuclear event? That's why they were underground.

Of course.

"Now, do you have anemia?"

She shook her head.

"Eczema?"

"No," she said as she glanced again at the empty doorway. Sizing up her escape plan.

Carter, completely unaware, continued. "Are you pregnant?"

Reggie snorted. "I thought I was once."

"That is irrelevant," he replied.

"Maybe to you." She smirked. "But it was the longest three weeks of my life."

He humorlessly looked down at the notepad again and tapped his pen on it.

She rolled her eyes. "No, I'm not damn pregnant."

Carter made another note. "Are you taking any medication?"

Reggie had enough. "Look, buddy, where's my sister? When is she getting here?"

Carter sighed.

Reggie could plainly see how tired this man was, not to mention how little he wanted to be in here with her.

He rubbed his eyes, and as he put his hand into his pocket, he pulled out a pair of sunglasses. Quickly putting them on, he carried on with his questions.

"Have you taken any medication in the last twenty-four hours?"

Reggie wasn't having any of it. "Shouldn't she be here by now? Even if Hector didn't show up? They were coming back, right? Where are they?"

Carter breathed loudly through his nose, with an expression of rapidly losing patience.

A knock on the open door stopped their conversation dead.

"Doctor Carter?" Wilson asked. "Can I speak to you for a moment?"

Carter immediately closed the notepad, put the pen in his jacket pocket, and stood. Before he left, he turned to Reggie and, with an infuriatingly calm voice said, "You should know. Your sister's dead."

For a second, the words didn't register. As if he had just told her it was going to rain tomorrow. But the words landed like a huge brick to her skull.

Her face started to wash with shock.

"Wh . . . what?"

Carter continued as he walked to the doorway. "I realize it's a shock," he said, devoid of emotion. "But she was exposed. Another forty-eight hours, and she would have died anyway. We did the humane thing. It was quite painless, I assure you."

With that, he was gone, the door shut behind him. He left Reggie, stuck in her mounting, distraught grief.

In this soundproof room, only she could hear the scream of anguish she then let out.

• • •

Carter stepped into the corridor, sliding his sunglasses off, rubbing his eyes again with his thumb and forefinger. They were sore. Very sore.

"What is it?" he asked. "What's so urgent it couldn't wait?"

Wilson looked anxious.

"Is it Audrey?" Carter asked. Somehow, sensing what happened.

"We lost radio contact with them," he said. "Last contact was from Oscar. He said Audrey was acting strange and would keep us updated."

Carter looked at him sharply. "Meaning?"

Wilson hesitated before he spoke. "We can't rule out the possibility that she may have gone into transition."

Carter swore under his breath. In a sudden burst of frustration, belying his cold exterior, he slammed his fist against the wall.

Wilson flinched, shocked at the reaction.

"We can't wait any longer," Carter snapped. "Let's just continue with what we have . . . Get the children done. Then this one." He jerked his thumb toward the door.

"But . . . there's not enough blood yet to last. How—"

"We are not robots, Doctor. We are not going to fall over all at once. Some will last a little longer." He paused, voice dropping. "While some of us have a more immediate need. Besides, if Audrey and Oscar do not return, that's less sustenance needed."

Wilson didn't argue, but he still looked worried.

"There's something else."

Carter shook his head. "Not now."

"It's important—it's about Rogers."

"The guard?"

Wilson nodded. "He hasn't been on duty for twenty-four hours now."

Carter didn't know what to say.

"We checked his quarters, and . . . it was turned upside down."

"What are you saying?"

"Rage . . . He may be infected."

The blood situation was bad enough, but a potentially infected guard running about?

The small examination room was just as white as the conference room Reggie was in. This room had the same fluorescent lighting. The same clinical sterility. The same coldness.

The two kids were sitting on a metal table in the middle of the room, their small legs swinging back and forth over the side. Davenport, a doctor in a white lab coat, was checking them over, moving methodically, pressing her stethoscope against their chests.

"You both have such nice, strong hearts," she said with a comforting smile.

The little girl frowned. "We're not gonna get shots, are we?"

Davenport smiled. "No, no shots. I promise."

The girl didn't look convinced.

· · ·

Reggie's hands were draped loosely over her lap, her expression bereft. Her eyes were bloodshot and face sagged.

The door opened with a click as Wilson stepped in.

He had the vibe of a high school counselor . . . like a guy who practiced his smile in the mirror but never got it right. And he was putting on his best sympathetic look, but Reggie wasn't buying it.

"I'm truly sorry about your sister, Regina," he said as he locked the door behind him, wary about the possible infected guard on the loose.

Reggie looked up slowly toward him but didn't react.

Didn't speak.

Didn't blink.

She just stared.

"Doctor Carter . . ." Wilson hesitated for a second. "Well, Doctor Carter . . . he's under a lot of pressure. He should have been gentler. Kinder. Explained everything."

Still, Reggie didn't move.

Wilson looked uneasy. "At any rate, I need you to come with me."

Reggie's gaze drifted down to the table.

Her voice, when it came, was dazed and distant. "The . . . ah . . . the table . . . it's broken."

"What?"

Reggie slowly reached forward and tipped the table by pushing on it.

It wobbled, then tilted unevenly as one of its legs, the one nearest to Reggie, was somehow missing.

Wilson frowned, puzzled. His concern was momentarily derailed by his confusion.

"What happened?" he asked as he leaned down, instinctively ducking his head beneath the table to see what she was talking about.

He never saw it coming.

In one fluid motion, Reggie stood, her fingers tightening around the table leg that had been unscrewed and hidden by her side. And with a sharp swing, she brought it crashing down against the back of Wilson's head.

With a dull, meaty crack, like a bat hitting wet sand, Wilson collapsed.

The corridor outside the conference room was empty.

Reggie opened the door and peered out, first looking one way, then the other.

The coast was clear.

She stepped into the corridor, moving quickly but carefully, keeping low as she followed the same path she had come in through.

She needed out.

And fast.

Outside the facility, the Nevada desert stretched into endless red-hued darkness. Little could be seen, but if it had been daytime, all the vistas would have exposed was an endless stretch of sand in all directions. The facility was truly in the middle of nowhere.

A guard stood by the razor-wire gate—Harrison, according to his name badge. He leaned against the gate, cigarette dangling from his lips, watching the night with the casual boredom once more. Before the world ended, this was just a cushy gig, guarding a bunker for rich weirdos. Turns out they weren't so crazy after all.

He may have hated the boredom and may not be getting paid anymore, but he was happy to be alive. Happy to be fed three times a day. Happy to have a warm bed, not to mention the endless supply of cigarettes they had here. There were many far worse outcomes a man like him could have faced.

That night was already a strange night—Rogers, his boss, had gone AWOL. And . . . what he hadn't expected to check off his bingo card was hearing "La Bamba" blaring from a Chevy Impala as it emerged from the darkness and rolled up to the gate.

He had been told to expect the two doctors back by car but not until the next day at the earliest.

Taking a slow drag of his cigarette, its orange glow flickering against the dark, he exhaled and dropped it to his feet, to the sand-covered asphalt.

In the car, the music thumped as the driver's side window suddenly wound down. A man in a loud floral shirt, with hair slicked back and a big smile, popped his head out as he turned the music low.

It was Hector Gomez.

"'Sup, my man?" he called out casually, his voice raised above the sound of the engine.

Unlike before, his accent was thick with a Latino twang, far from his usual West-Coast drawl.

Harrison slowly reached for his sidearm, resting his fingers against the holster as he stepped forward. This was not who he was expecting.

"Who are you?" he demanded. "Name and purpose."

Hector grinned. "I'm Hector Gomez, ése."

He pushed the driver's side door open and stepped out, stretching his legs and taking a deep breath of the warm desert air in. The Impala continued to idle behind him as Ritchie Valens crooned quietly through the speakers.

He looked Harrison up and down. "Bitchin' ropa, dude," he said with a friendly smirk, motioning to his uniform. "What are you guys, Freedom Fighters or somethin'? Viva Ché and all that shit?"

Harrison didn't laugh. His stare remained cold and very suspicious.

"How did you find this place?" he said.

Hector paused as if suddenly remembering why he was there.

"Oh, yeah. This lady back in L.A. sent me—Audrey, I think her name was. A doc from here?"

Harrison relaxed at hearing her name.

Hector continued, "You been to L.A. lately? It's all fucked up, man. The city's a goddamn ghost town. But anyway . . . I came here to show you somethin'. She told me to."

He turned, walking toward the trunk of his car, continuing to chatter as he went. "You know what the

Harbor Freeway's usually like? Torture to drive? Bumper to bumper, right? Well, you can drive a hundred miles an hour there now. The roads are nearly empty. And on Van Nuys Boulevard? You can drive on the damn sidewalks. It's heavy, man!"

By now, they had both reached the back of the car.

Harrison was still suspicious, so he kept his hand resting on his gun, watching every step this stranger took.

Suddenly, Hector's entire demeanor changed. His casual attitude dropped, replaced by something lower, quieter, and secretive. He glanced around, checking for people listening, then leaned into the guard.

"Hey, man," he said. "D'you like girls?"

"What are you talking about?"

Hector reached for the trunk lid and popped it open with a quiet click. "Look in here."

Harrison looked down and gasped.

The body of Samantha Belmont was curled inside the trunk.

For a horrible moment, Harrison didn't know what to do. "Is she dead?" he asked in disbelief.

To which Hector laughed out loud. "Dead? Nah, man!"

Confused and slightly curious, Harrison leaned in to get a closer look, squinting at Samantha in the low light.

"That lady I told you about. The one who told me to come here? She gave my girl here a shot of sodium pentothal . . . to make this other dude who was from here think that she was dead." Hector's smile dropped.

"'Cause, she didn't want any of you assholes to get hold of her blood . . ."

Before Harrison could turn—

Samantha moved.

Her eyes snapped open.

Her hand shot out.

She grabbed the guard by the collar, yanking him forward just as—

SLAM.

Hector brought the trunk lid down on his head in a single, brutal, well-coordinated move.

The metal crashed against Harrison, knocking him unconscious.

Hector then let out a low, satisfied exhale. As he dropped his fake accent. "Fuckin' vampire freaks."

The corridors were straight and seemingly endless, with all doors flush to the walls, almost invisible until you got close to them.

Reggie moved quickly and carefully, not seeing anyone, desperate to draw no undue attention.

She kept going over all that had been said. All that she had heard. What did the doctor say? Twenty people and security staff? So . . . thirty maybe? From the size of this facility, that seemed like a tiny number. Maybe she wouldn't even see another person on her way out. That is *if* she found her way out. But she had already resigned herself to the fact that escape may be impossible, as she had no idea where she was. Her memory of the way she was brought in was wrong. In the panic, in her grief, she could not remember her lefts from her rights. She was lost.

As she stepped down the corridor, she could feel the weight of every door as she passed, convinced each one would open to reveal someone with a gun lunging at her.

Then, making her jump, the facility's PA system came to life, uncomfortably loud.

"Facility . . ."

It was Wilson's voice. He sounded distracted and pained. As he carried on speaking, his voice carried with it a small waver. A tremble.

"Everyone . . . our adolescent guest has escaped."

Adolescent?! She was eighteen years old, goddamnit. Sure, she had three more years to drinking age, but did that matter? Did any of it matter?

She slowed down and thought for a minute. She needed a plan of action.

She would . . . She . . .

In silence, she mouthed, *Shit*.

She had no element of surprise. They must have found the guy she hit with the table leg, or he woke up . . . They were looking for her. She should have hit him way harder, then hid the body.

On the PA, Carter kept on talking, his voice rolling through the speakers. "She . . . she's quite hostile . . . And she may have already gone topside. We cannot, under any circumstances, allow her to leave."

As she came to a junction, Reggie turned sharply left. No rhyme or reason. She just had to go in one direction, and taking any time deciding would have been a waste. She had no idea where she was, so she just had to keep moving.

Coming up ahead, she saw an open door. Slowing, she started to hear voices. The sound of people moving.

She didn't stop to dwell. Without missing a beat, she spun on her heels, then backtracked the way she came, trying each door she could along the way. Knowing that someone was about to walk out.

The first door was locked.

Locked.

Locked.

Crossing the corridor intersection, she carried on ahead but picked up speed.

Locked.

Locked.

Open!

She slipped in as quickly as she could, shutting it quietly behind her.

Even outside the compound, the PA continued through the perimeter fence speakers.

"Everyone, please. Take a moment to look around you. She must be caught."

Hurriedly walking through the gate, with the flood-lights illuminating the area, Hector made his way over toward the row of utility vehicles, hugging the fence to ensure he was not seen by anyone else who may be around. In his hands, he carried a full gas canister as well as sticks of dynamite.

· · ·

The second Reggie was inside the dark room, she pressed her back to the cold metal wall and tried her best to control her breathing. To stop herself from breaking down. If she got out of this place, there would be time to mourn. Now, though, she just had to focus. She had to push her memories of Samantha as far down as she could.

In this dark, she could tell from the cooler air and the sound of the ventilation far away that it was a large space. Much larger than the room from before.

"Look in each one," she heard from the corridor outside.

Faint but audible. Then the sound of heavy footsteps. Men in boots. Two of them, walking with purpose.

She heard a door open.

Then close.

Then a nearer one.

She stayed perfectly still, straining her ears.

"I said check them all," one of them said. "What about that one?"

"Aw, I hate that room," the other replied. "Swear they look at you."

"Just do it!"

She knew immediately they were talking about this room. *But who were they?*

Quickly, she lowered herself to the floor and crawled blindly across the floor, until she came to what felt like a metal table.

She rushed around to the other side and kept low as the door creaked open and a guard walked in.

She closed her eyes and stopped breathing.

The light from the corridor did nothing to illuminate where she was, but for the guard looking in, it was enough to make out most of the room.

He walked in a few feet and paused, lingering, scanning the whole space.

"Anything?" the other guard asked, peering in from the corridor.

"Nothing but the blood bags," replied the one staring.

For one tense moment, nothing happened.

"Gives me the damn creeps," he added, just before the door clicked again and the little light that was in here vanished.

Reggie waited a few seconds before releasing the breath she had been holding. Slowly, she got to her feet.

The room was cloaked in darkness, faintly illuminated by the dull glow of a nearby bank of computer monitors. As his eyes adjusted, more became clear. That's when she saw them . . .

Bodies.

Naked, uncovered bodies.

Half a dozen of them lay upside down on tilted medical tables. Their mouths were wide open, their bodies in their shackles. Tubes ran from their veins, draining into large glass containers below.

Reggie was at once horrified yet fascinated as she willed herself to step forward. She wasn't squeamish, but this . . . this was something else.

She moved closer to one of the bodies. Staring at the blood being taken. The slow, steady drip, drip, drip that traveled from the needle in their arms, along a long plastic tube and down into the container.

"My God . . ." she whispered, noticing the nearby life support machines.

Her stomach turned.

They were alive and being bled.

She took a step closer. She had to see if she could help. Maybe she could untie them.

But then she was grabbed.

An arm locked around her throat, pulling her back with terrifying strength.

She gasped, and her hands flew up and clawed at this sudden grip.

The lights in the room suddenly flooded on, blindingly bright, making her wince.

It was the guards. They had played a trick on her. They knew she was in there and had pretended to leave. It was all an act.

The door then swung open, and standing there without any emotional expression was Wilson.

He didn't look surprised. He didn't even look angry, even though the wound on his head still was trickling blood down his shirt. He just adjusted his glasses like a disappointed parent.

"Good," he said. "We found you."

Reggie tried to struggle free as she was dragged to the door, but the guard's hold on her was too firm.

Wilson barely even looked at her as she came near. He simply turned and left the room ahead of her, leading the way.

The other guard by the light switch smiled at her victoriously as she kicked and clawed ineffectually.

Outside, Hector lay on his back beneath one of the utility vehicles, working as quickly as he could. His fingers twisted wire after wire together, and a small grin was fixed on his face. He needed to work fast and, more importantly, remain unseen.

Just as he finished and was about to slide under the next vehicle, he had heard it.

The click of a door opening, then closing shut.

Under the vehicle, he slowly turned his head, straining to see who it was and what direction they were walking in.

Then came the footsteps. Heavy and slow. Each step was accompanied by deep, labored breathing.

Hector steadied his breath as a pair of camouflage-patterned trousered legs moved past him, only inches from the vehicle he hid behind.

They then stopped.

The boots remained still, their owner just standing there, breathing those slow, deep breaths.

Hector couldn't tell if it was a man or a woman. But he didn't care. They were all the enemy here.

Finally, they moved on. Dragging their feet behind them as they walked.

The two young children sat next to each other on the metal examination table. Dressed in the same white gowns as earlier, both were quiet and looking nervously at each other.

Beside them, two massive gas cylinders stood upright, clearly labeled *carbon monoxide*. Trailing from one of the cylinders, a thin tube coiled across to a facemask. A facemask held by Davenport, the doctor, smiling kindly at them.

Next to her, an assistant called Minder stood by, watching with an almost identical smile.

"Nothing to be worried about," Davenport said reassuringly to the children.

Just then, the door opened, and Carter entered. Still wearing his sunglasses. "Everything's now under control," he said. "I just got word that they have the girl and are bringing her down now."

Davenport barely reacted. "Good," she said as she turned back to the kids, her voice turning softer. "Okay, I'm going to put this mask over your noses and mouths," she said, leaning in. "I just want you to breathe in *very* deeply, alright?"

The boy frowned as he looked at her. "But you said no shots."

"This isn't a shot, sweetheart," she replied with a smile. "This will just make you sleepy."

Minder nodded. "That's right. And when you wake up, do you know where you'll be?"

The children looked unsure.

"Where?" the little girl finally asked.

Minder smiled, an unconvincing, creepy smile. "Disneyland."

The kids' eyes lit up.

"Really?"

"Yes, indeed," Minder replied. "Mickey, Minnie, and Goofy will all be there."

Davenport started to raise the mask toward the boy.

"But . . . they're not real," he suddenly said, knowing better than to believe this fantastical offer. "They're just cartoons, and cartoons are not real."

"Oh, they are *very* real," Carter added from the doorway.

"Well, my mom said they weren't," the boy persisted.

"Hush now and breathe in, okay?" Davenport urged. "You'll not only be going to Disneyland . . . you'll then be going to the North Pole to see Santa Claus."

The girl smiled happily as her tiny hands fidgeted in excitement.

The boy, though, did not. He looked worried. But he did not have the bravery to complain as Davenport lowered the mask over his face.

The door to a building was open. The sign on it was printed in bold black lettering.

Generator Room

High Voltage

Danger of Death

Inside, a large bank of machines hummed with the flow of the electricity, sending it throughout the complex.

The main controller for the generators had one

emergency shut-off lever. A lever whose plastic safety stopper was now broken on the floor. The one thing stopping any accidental cut-offs.

But with Hector there, this was no accident. Not as he reached up and pulled the large lever down . . .

. . . The power then went out across the whole underground facility.

Just as Davenport was about to fix the mask on the boy's face, the room was plunged into a sudden darkness. The bright white overhead strip lighting was immediately replaced by the dull orange glow of emergency backup systems.

Carter immediately stopped, his eyes darting up to the lights.

In the corridor, the sound of alarms tripped and wailed through the facility like a police siren.

With a toothy grunt, Carter grimaced as his stony demeanor fractured.

"The life support!" he snapped.

Minder's face paled. "Oh my god, no!"

"Don't worry, the backup generators will kick in soon," Davenport reassured.

But that was not good enough for Carter, who didn't wait. He was already turning out of the door.

"They won't last that long!" he said sharply.

As he rushed out, the boy blinked in confusion.

"Hey," he said. "What about Disneyland?"

· · ·

Carter stormed into the corridor, nearly running into Wilson and the guards that held Reggie. Here, the emergency lights were just as weak as inside the room. Not that it bothered Carter, as he *still* wore his sunglasses.

"With me," he barked to Wilson.

"What about the girl?"

Carter waved dismissively. "Put her with the others. They can all be put down."

As the two guards nodded, Carter was gone, having stormed down the corridor with Wilson at his heels.

Reggie watched in silence as she saw them go, her mind already working through a plan that she had to enact *right now*.

With all her strength, she threw her entire weight backward, slamming into his ribs as they crashed against the wall.

His grip loosened just enough for her to twist her arms free.

She drove her elbow into his throat with a battle cry.

Gasping for air, he staggered back, choking.

The other guard lunged forward, but Reggie managed to duck, missing his arms. She whirled around and punched him hard on the temple, knocking him unconscious in a single clean punch. A punch that resulted in a shot of awful pain through her knuckles. The price for such an effective hit.

But Reggie didn't stop. She dropped low to the first guard, sending a sharp kick to his solar plexus as he tried to breathe. It knocked the rest of the wind out of him. As he doubled over, she swung her balled fist upward. An uppercut that laid him out cold on the floor next to his colleague.

With them both out, she grabbed their revolvers, holding one in each hand.

She was almost ready to break her way out with guns blazing. *Almost.*

Before she turned to run away, she hesitated. Something made her glance back toward the open room Carter came from. Inside, she saw the dull glow of the emergency lighting.

Edging closer to the doorway, she peeked inside.

There was a slow, mechanical hiss of gas being pumped through the facemask as Davenport and Minder carried on with their work. Fixing the mask over the boy's face, Davenport was totally oblivious to what had happened in the corridor.

Without considering any potential consequences, Reggie stepped into the room, both guns raised.

"Hey, fuckos!" she said loudly.

Startled, Davenport spun to face her as Minder, who was on the other side of the examination table, tensed.

The boy under the mask blinked, wide-eyed, and said in a small, innocent voice, "They said if we breathe this, we get to go to Disneyland."

Reggie gritted her teeth.

Disneyland?

"Take it off!" she said urgently.

As the boy pulled the mask off his own mouth, neither Davenport nor Minder spoke up or tried to fight. They did not have the nerve to, not with a gun being pointed at each of them.

Reggie took a step closer, leveling both guns' aim directly at Davenport's chest. "Step away from the kid. *Now.*"

But before anyone could move, a shadow fell over the doorway behind them, causing Davenport to glance past Reggie in confusion.

"Hey," a voice said happily.

Immediately, Reggie turned, her guns leading her way as her fingers pulled tight on the triggers.

She fired both guns.

The bullets tore through the air, smashed into the doorframe, splintering the wood, just as the shadow dropped to the floor. Narrowly avoiding the shots, their hands flew up in surrender.

"Holy shit! I give! I give!" the voice added.

Reggie froze.

It took her half a second to realize who she was looking at.

Samantha.

Her sister.

Alive.

Very much alive.

Reggie could only stare. A dozen emotions rushed through her in rapid succession. Relief, shock, confusion, happiness. But there was no time for a tearful reunion.

She turned back to Davenport and Minder, gun raised at them once more.

"They told me you were dead," Reggie said, without looking back.

"Yeah, well, they are lying sacks of shit," Samantha

replied as she stood.

Reggie kept her gaze firmly on the doctors. "Get your hands up now," she ordered.

Without hesitation, both complied. Holding their hands up high.

At the same time, the two kids on the table, having watched this scene unfold, mirrored them, lifting their hands as well.

"Not you two," Reggie said, with a sudden, unexpected laugh. "You can put your hands down."

"Who are you?" the boy asked.

"I'm . . . I'm . . . uhhh . . . Aunt Regina," Reggie said, having no idea how to talk to kids. "And this is Aunt Samantha." She smiled at them as the guns were still aimed at the doctors. "What are your names?"

"I'm Brian," the boy said.

"Sarah," the girl added quietly.

Reggie gave a small nod. "Alright, Brian, Sarah. We're getting out of here. Okay?"

Samantha stepped up and nodded toward Davenport and Minder. "What about them?"

Reggie thought for a moment as a slow smirk crept onto her face. "A taste of their own medicine."

In the room where the six bodies were being drained, with their blood siphoned away as the machines around them kept them on the precipice of life, Carter and Wilson were working frantically. The bodies were no longer tilted up but instead lying flat on the tables. Both doctors were trying to salvage what little life remained. The power outage had shut off the life support systems and had been the only thing keeping the bodies from slipping away completely.

"It's useless," Wilson sighed as he stopped chest compressions on one of the bodies. "We've lost them . . . All of them."

Carter, though, was still compressing one of the bodies' chests frantically, desperate for his efforts to work. But after another twenty seconds, he slowly stopped. Coming to the same conclusion as Wilson. It *was* useless.

Perspiring and out of breath from his effort, Carter was thinking aloud. "We can start over, with those children and that girl. Only three of them . . . well, the kids really only count as one full human, but two is enough until we find more." He motioned to the bodies on the tables. "We'll drain the rest of these. And we have some stock left that will last us a short while."

Wilson looked worried, wanting to believe Carter but fearing for the worse.

Samantha, Reggie and the kids moved quickly, not caring to mask the sounds of their urgent footsteps. The corridor stretched ahead of them, dimly lined by the orange emergency lights glowing along the ceiling.

Reggie had hold of one of the guard's revolvers as Samantha had the other. She glanced behind them, making sure they weren't being followed.

Soon reaching the elevator, she slammed on the

call button with the hilt of her gun. It was only a matter of seconds before the doors slid open with a soft hiss.

"This thing still work?" Samantha asked. "There's no power."

Reggie shrugged. "The doors opened, so I guess they're fine?"

The kids were the first of them to scramble into the elevator, pressing themselves against the back wall, their hands still raised like prisoners awaiting sentencing. Thinking this was all some big fun joke.

"Put 'em down, kids," Reggie said, rolling her eyes, trying to play along and not scare them. "Don't be so stupid."

Carter and Wilson stormed into the examination room, fully expecting to find the two kids and Reggie being held by the guards.

But that is not what they found.

The operating table was occupied but not by who they were expecting to see.

Davenport and Minder were strapped down, their hands and feet bound tightly, using their lab coats as rope. Gas masks had been placed over their faces, the steady hiss of airflow coming from the carbon monoxide canisters. A taste of their own medicine, indeed. They weren't dead yet, but both struggled weakly, barely able to move.

On the floor beneath them, the two guards lay in an unconscious heap. Weapons missing.

Pinned to the table was a hand-scrawled note on one of the doctors' notepads.

Gone to Disneyland without you.

The sardonic note only served to infuriate the already angry Carter.

His hands clenched. His jaw twitched as a rage bubbled beneath the surface but not just a normal rage.

Wilson, on the other hand, almost looked amused by the ridiculousness of the situation.

That humor only made Carter more furious. He exhaled through gritted teeth, his gaze lifting toward the ceiling as if envisioning where Reggie and the kids were by now.

"Get everyone topside. *Now*," he seethed at Wilson. "We will block the gates."

Wilson motioned with his head to Minder and Wilson. "But shouldn't we help them out first?"

Carter shook his head in disgust. "Let them go. Fewer to divide the blood among." His glare turned terrifying. "Don't you want that, Wilson?"

But Wilson had no idea what he wanted anymore. It was all unraveling too fast.

Outside, the nighttime desert air was getting colder.

The fenced-in top level of the facility was still lit by the harsh glare of the floodlights, joined by rotating yellow emergency beacons, whose pale beams swept across the compound in a spinning rhythm, casting long, shifting shadows across the sandy concrete ground.

The door to one of the blockhouses that housed the elevator quickly opened, and Reggie, Samantha, and the kids hurried out.

The moment they did, a pair of headlights flicked on and shined blindingly at them, causing them to stop in their tracks.

Reggie raised her gun at the light in sudden fear, but Samantha pushed it back down as she smiled. "It's for us!"

An engine roared as the Impala pulled to a stop in front of them.

Hector, with one arm slung out the window, grinned like he had all the time in the world.

"Hey there, beautiful people," he said. "You order a taxi?"

Reggie didn't have time for small talk. She yanked open the car door, ushering the kids inside. Samantha got in with them.

"The kids with us?" Hector asked.

"Where the hell have you been?" Reggie asked, getting in the passenger seat, annoyed that Samantha was sent into the facility on her own.

"I've been arranging a barbecue for your friends. Found some presents for them in their storehouse."

With that, he flicked on the radio as the strains of Ritchie Valens came over the speakers.

Samantha groaned, pressing a hand to her temple. "I really hate this music."

"Move it, now!" Reggie urged.

Hector didn't need to be told twice.

"Hold on to your butts," he exclaimed.

The Impala kicked up clouds of sand as it sped through the compound and out of the front gate but, when outside, came to a quick stop.

"What are you doing?" Reggie asked.

Staring in his side mirror, Hector had seen the blockhouse door open again.

"There they are! *Get them*!" Carter exclaimed as he saw the Impala at the gate.

Along with Wilson and a handful of guards, they headed straight to the utility vehicles.

From the driver's side window, Hector poked his head out. With no hesitation, no fear, and absolutely zero concern for self-preservation, he grinned like an idiot and called out, "Hey, come on, guys! You're supposed to be such hot shit! Try and catch us! Come on, I dare ya!"

Carter stiffened. His entire body was coiled with red-hot anger as he screamed. "Catch them! Catch them all now!"

"C'mon, chicken shits!" Hector hollered. He flapped one arm out of the window like a wing, his other hand cupped around his mouth as he mimicked a chicken.

"Buck, buck, buuuuuuck!"

His taunt echoed to Carter's ears, who roared back at them.

Reggie was looking worried out of the back window. "Are you out of your mind? We gotta get out of here!"

Without looking back, Hector replied, "Trust me, this is gonna be a whole heap of awesome."

Just to drive his point home, he slapped his hand against the control panel under the dash. With a sharp hiss of air, the car's air suspension shocks kicked in, and the Impala lurched upward, bouncing once before settling high on its axles. He laughed as he hit the switch again. The shocks released, and the Impala dropped back down hard, its nose dipping dramatically before popping back up.

The kids in the back laughed like it was a fairground ride.

Carter raced into the passenger seat of the first utility vehicle. Wilson was already at the wheel. He watched enraged as the Impala jumped on its front wheels beyond the fence. Taking off his sunglasses, he rubbed his eyes hard, the pain in his head burning his sight.

As Wilson put his hand on the ignition key, he suddenly paused. Something was amiss.

He took a breath in through his nose.

"Do you smell that?" he asked.

But Carter could not hear him over his own anger. Something was taking over him. A metamorphosis.

"Do you?" Wilson asked.

"Stop talking!" Carter hissed as he turned to Wilson with a smile twitching up his face. "I want their blood!"

His eyes had turned completely white, blotting out his pupils and irises. In seconds, the blood ran from his face, leaving a deathly white pallor.

As Wilson gasped, Carter lunged at him, letting out a violent growl like an enraged cat.

Backing away, terrified, Wilson grabbed the door handle and fell out of the vehicle, landing on the ground outside, escaping Carter's clutches.

Aiming a frenzied gaze on the Impala, Carter's attention turned from Wilson as he suddenly grabbed the ignition and twisted the key. He wanted the people who got away. He wanted to rip them to pieces. He wanted to eat their still-warm flesh. He wanted to—

CHAPTER
EIGHT

THE ROW of utility vehicles stood in perfect formation near the fenced-in entrance to the underground facility, their metal frames gleaming under the floodlights.

In an instant, the first explosion tore through the night.

Carter's vehicle was the first to go up.

The dynamite wired into the ignition flared with a blinding flash, turning the entire truck into a blistering fireball. The violent blast ripped through the chassis as if it were paper.

Wilson, who had fallen out of the vehicle moments before, was still scrambling to get away from the mutated Carter, but he did not get far. As the blast hit him full force, it swallowed him up, engulfing his body before he could even scream. Incinerating him to the bone marrow.

Like a chain of dominos, the rest of the vehicles followed suit.

The dynamite beneath each one detonated in rapid

succession, a rolling thunder of explosions that rampaged through the compound, turning them each into flying shrapnel and incinerated corpses.

But the real inferno then erupted from below.

The gasoline-soaked sand, that waited for the explosions like a trap, ignited all at once, sending columns of fire twisting into the air. The heat was instant and all-consuming, turning the entire area into a raging wall of flame.

The whole compound was soon bathed in hellish light.

From beyond the open gate as the raging inferno reflected in the rear windscreen of the Chevy Impala, its doors slowly opened.

Gone was the mocking smirk as Hector stepped out with a shocked expression.

Reggie and Samantha got out, too, all three speechless and mesmerized by the sight.

Even the kids, Brian and Sarah, huddled in the backseat, stuck their heads up just enough to peer through the glass, terrified but too curious not to watch.

For a while, no one spoke.

Until . . .

"Wow . . . alright, Hector," Samantha murmured, her voice almost lost beneath the sound of the flames. "You made your damn point."

"Yeah," he said. "I didn't expect it to be *that* big."

Reggie's gaze remained locked on the fire. "Is this

what our lives are now? All killing? That . . . That's gonna be a drag."

"Nah, it won't. The lady who told me where you were said anyone even a little bit infected would be gone by the end of the week. After that, all monsters will be gone."

Reggie didn't say anything back.

None of them did as each realized that applied to them, too. If any of them had even a hint of an infection from the comet, they would not see out the rest of the week.

Instead of voicing their worry, they just watched as the compound burned as the smoke began to rise in thick black columns into the cold red sky.

It was eerily peaceful. And just as that sense of calm began to settle—

A shape roared and smashed through the car window, reaching for the kids in the back seat.

The man's face, decimated by the fire, let out a ravenous roar. Even in his torn, ripped, and bloody state, it was obviously one of the guards. The name badge was barely legible but could just be made out, *Rogers*.

The missing guard.

Somehow, he was still standing. Having been stumbling nearby, he had been caught in the billowing flames, and he only had one thing on his mind. Blood.

His ruined body staggered forward, hunger overriding his pain. His milky eyes locked onto the youngest of the group in the back seat of the Impala. The easiest prey.

Brian and Sarah screamed as the window shattered.

Reggie, Samantha, and Hector turned around just as the hellish vision of Rogers reached inside the car. His half-incinerated arms grabbed blindly for the kids.

"Blood!" he cried in gargle. "*Blood!*"

Sarah cried out, kicking wildly as she scrambled into the front seat, while Brian was yanked halfway out of the window, trying to grab at the window frame.

Reggie was already moving.

She threw herself into the backseat through the other side, latching onto Brian's legs, just as Rogers's rotting fingers dug into the fabric of the boy's shirt.

"Sammy! Help Sarah!" Reggie shouted, fighting against the monstrous grip as Rogers not only pulled Brian out of the car but dragged her halfway out, too.

Meanwhile, Samantha opened the driver's side door as Sarah scrambled out into her arms.

Hector moved quickly around the car, gun drawn, but couldn't get a clear shot, as Reggie was half out of the car, blocking his shot.

"Get out of the way!" he shouted.

Reggie gritted her teeth, then yanked as hard as she could, but Rogers had a vise-like grip on the child.

"What the hell do you think I'm trying to do?!" she snapped back.

"*Blood!*" Rogers gurgled again.

Brian cried out in fear and pain, his body almost pulled from Reggie's grasp.

Hector had no choice.

He had to get in close.

He stepped forward, pressed the barrel of his gun against Rogers's temple, and pulled the trigger.

BANG.

The gunshot tore through the guard's brain, ringing in everyone's ears as his head jerked violently to the side.

The force of the shot sent him sprawling onto the desert ground, his grip finally releasing on Brian, who tumbled back into Reggie's arms.

But Hector wasn't done. He had seen too many films where the bad guy got up again.

He took two steps closer and fired again. Once into Rogers's chest, then once more for good measure.

Then another in the head.

Then another.

Then . . . *CLICK.*

The bullets were out, and there was no way Rogers could get up from this.

As the sounds of the loud gunshots dissipated and the roar of the fires behind them began to settle, the only sound left was Sarah's quiet sobs as she clung to Samantha. Her small fingers gripped Samantha's shirt like it was a lifeline.

Reggie pulled Brian into the car. He began to cry as well as the shock gave way to his upset.

"Alright, kid," she said softly into his ear. "You're okay. We're all gonna be okay."

Soon, everyone was back in the car, and Hector began the long drive back to L.A. Behind them, the sun had started to rise.

As they hit Interstate 15, both kids were asleep in

the back seat, huddled against Samantha, who had drifted off with them. Her head lolled back as she snored with her mouth.

Reggie turned in her seat, watching them for a moment. They looked so at peace, tucked into each other like a makeshift family. It didn't seem fair. They shouldn't have had to go through any of this, Samantha included. But here they were.

She smiled an uncertain, uneasy smile. Was she even ready for this? Watching over her sister was one thing, as she'd been doing that for years. But these two? They were more than just survivors. They were kids. Kids who needed someone to protect them.

The thought pressed down on her, heavier than she expected.

She exhaled softly and leaned back. Ready or not, they were hers now.

"It'll be okay," Hector said quietly, seeing her silent confusion. "Whatever happens, we'll all get by."

For the rest of the journey, no one spoke.

No one needed to.

They had survived.

They just had to survive the week, and beyond that, they had to survive the new world that waited for them.

As the days drifted into weeks and the season started to end, the red haze that had smothered the western seaboard of what was now the Desolate States of America began to lift. What felt like a permanent smog, draped over every building and street, slowly faded with each passing sunrise. The comet's dust trail that stained the sky like a blood streak had dispersed into nothing, leaving behind it a crystal blue expanse. The world itself started to look normal again.

Even if life could not say the same.

Down Rodeo Drive, two small figures stood outside a high-end boutique.

Brian shifted uncomfortably in a suit and tie, tugging at the collar like it was strangling him. Next to him, Sarah practically radiated unbridled joy as she twirled in front of the boutique's shattered display window. The silk frills on her party dress billowed as she spun. Before the world fell, neither would have ever been able to wear these clothes due to the extortionate price tags.

Brian frowned, stuffing his small hands in his pockets. "Do I really have to wear this?"

Sarah still turned, beaming. "I love my dress!"

"You look so cute!" Reggie shrieked with delight. "Don't move!"

Coming to a stop, Sarah reached out, held her brother's hand, and gave a big smile to the camera.

With a click and a whir, Reggie put down the Polaroid camera and looked at the kids happily.

Reggie, herself, was also transformed, having raided a nearby boutique herself. Not an Yvonne St. Lawrence knock-off, as Doris would have worn, but the real thing. An exquisite evening dress, along with pearl accessories and heels.

"One more," she asked the kids as she raised the camera again.

"Do we *have* to?" Brian complained.

Reggie laughed as she looked up from the camera. "Come on, for me?"

That one more photo soon turned into ten.

Farther up the street, Hector and Samantha peered into the trash can in front of them.

Hector was sporting an expensive jacket and tie, but Samantha had skipped the Rodeo Drive look all together. While the others raided boutiques, she grabbed jeans and a T-shirt from a Kmart sale rack. Clothes that felt more . . . like her.

"I think this is a mistake," she said, staring down at the handguns that had been thrown away.

Hector shrugged. "Talk to your sister. She doesn't want the kids near any guns."

Samantha turned and peered up the street, watching as Reggie crouched, camera in hand, snapping pictures of the kids. For a fleeting moment, she looked different. Not just like their makeshift guardian but like a real mom. A loving mom.

"But what if we find someone else . . . and they're not nice?"

Hector casually gestured toward the bulky U-Haul trailer hitched to the back of the stretched limo parked behind them.

"We won't need guns," he said. "We need what's in there . . . stuff to trade. Videos, records, toilet paper, food. Anything, really . . . And besides, this city isn't exactly short on firepower. If we really need 'em, we'll find more guns."

He paused, then motioned farther toward the street. "Heads up."

Samantha followed his gaze.

Reggie was finished with the photoshoot and was walking back over to them, a kid holding onto each of her hands.

"I really can't believe this shit," she said. "Reggie Belmont, mother of the fucking world."

Hector chuckled. "Watch your language."

Samantha nodded. "Yeah, yeah, not around the kids. I know." She turned back to him. "You know, you guys look like *I Love Lucy*, don't you?"

"Hey, the responsibility of civilization has fallen to us. Better *I Love Lucy* than *Hill Street Blues*." He paused for a beat before smiling. "You know, we can make this world so much *better* than it was."

"Don't put that stress on me. I don't wanna break out in any more rashes!"

Reggie was standing with the kids at the pedestrian crossing. Waiting for the green traffic light to turn red.

Samantha looked at them, baffled. "What the hell—I mean, what the *heck* are you doing?"

Reggie smiled. "Waiting for the light to change. Can't cross the road against the light. That's dangerous."

Samantha searched for something intelligent to say, but all that came out was, "Are you nuckin' futz?"

"Hey! We *don't* cross against the light," Reggie said pointedly.

Without looking either way down the street, Samantha stepped into the road toward them. Trying to make a point. This was not before. The same rules can't apply.

"Auntie Regina," she said. "Do please beg my pardon when I tell you that is totally stupid."

At that very second, as if fated by the galaxy to prove a point, a bright yellow Triumph TR7 rounded the corner. Its roar only heard as it careened by, almost running Samantha over.

She only just managed to jump out of its way in time.

It roared away down the street into the distance.

No one had expected that, and everyone turned to stare after it.

"H-How . . . We searched the city for weeks, and only now, right at this *exact* moment, does someone appear . . . in a car. To prove me fucking wrong?"

Reggie turned to the kids with a smile. "And that is why we never cross against the light."

Down the street, the TR7 reappeared, backing up toward them, until it came to a stop in front of the pedestrian crossing.

Hector moved his hand over the trash can, waiting to grab out one of the discarded weapons. Not believing his own spiel about trade now that he was faced with meeting someone new.

From the TR7, a young devastatingly handsome teenage boy got out, with a relieved smile.

"People!" he said loudly. "I'm so damn glad to see *people*! I'm Danny! Uhh . . . Danny Mason Keener. I can't believe it! Finally! *PEOPLE!*"

Samantha could not believe her eyes. Glancing skyward, she lightly mouthed *Thank you* to whatever deity, alien, or comet had now decided to answer her prayers.

Hector's eyes narrowed. He was not sure he trusted this guy yet, but he moved his hand away from the trash can and walked over.

"I'm Hector," he said, trying to act older and more in charge than he really was.

"I'm happy to meet ya, dude!" Danny replied.

"I'm Reggie," she said. "This is Brian and Sarah."

"It's a pleasure! This is so *awesome!*"

Danny was clearly over the moon, as he had not seen another human in many, many weeks. Not since the comet.

He turned to Samantha. "And what's your name?"

Not hearing the question, she just giggled and said the only thing she could think of. "Nice car."

"Uh, well, hello there Ms. Nice Car," Danny laughed.

"I mean Samantha. My name is Samantha. Sammy. Sam . . . But you have a nice car?"

Danny motioned to the TR7. "This old thing? Ah, it's okay. I got about so many better ones." He paused before asking. "Don't suppose you wanna take a ride?"

She turned to Hector, for some reason looking for permission from him.

Hector looked over to Reggie. "Hey, can Samantha go for a ride with this young guy?" he called out.

Reggie smiled. "Sure, but she has to be back by midnight!"

Samantha's stomach knotted with embarrassment.

Hector leaned in nearer to her and repeated the message. "You have to be back by midnight, little missy."

Samantha spoke softly behind a fake smile. "Fuck you."

Hector let out a laugh as she walked over to Danny. He called out after them. "Be sure to keep to the speed limit."

Danny turned to her, puzzled. "What did he say?"

She shrugged. "The responsibility of the whole of human civilization has fallen on us or some shit."

Danny smiled. "Oh, yeah. Bitchin', isn't it?"

As they got in the TR7 and started to drive away, Regina caught sight of its vanity plate. There it was . . . in large bold letters.

DMK.

The interloper.

She could not help but laugh.

After a few moments, as the traffic lights turned red and the green crossing light flashed, she and the kids looked both ways up the street before walking over to Hector.

"She's gonna be okay, right?" he asked. "We just let her get in a stranger's car."

"Oh, I'm way more worried about him with her. He doesn't stand a chance."

Life, such as it was as unreal as it felt, moved forward.

Day after day, the world changed, yet somehow, it remained the same.

Above, the sky stretched wide, blue and open, the sun casting its golden light over the hollow streets of the City of Angels.

There was no more dust.

No more strange red glow.

No more monsters lurking in the shadows.

Not even any bodies to remind them of the deaths.

Just empty streets, scattered clothes and the echoes of a world that had once been full.

This was a city waiting to be reclaimed in a world waiting to be explored.

And somewhere, out there in the silence, there were other survivors to find.

Regina, Samantha, Hector, Brian, Sarah, and Danny . . . This hapless band . . . They would live as if the world had never ended.

AFTER THE COMET

BY CATHERINE MARY STEWART
AND KELLI MARONEY

When *Night of the Comet* premiered in 1984, it arrived like a B-movie meteor, wild, unexpected, and unforgettable. On the surface, it was a modestly budgeted sci-fi comedy about a comet wiping out most of humanity. But at its heart, it was something more: a film where two young women weren't waiting to be rescued — they were leading the charge.

Kelli Maroney knew the film was special the moment she read it. "I laughed my butt off. It was so funny. I was actually on a plane reading the script and laughing out loud," she said. "People around me were kind of like looking at me, like I was crazy, but I just thought it was hilarious."

For Catherine Mary Stewart, it was the originality that stood out. "It captured so many different genres. It was unique. It was quirky. "Another element that attracted me to the movie was the character of Regina. Up until then I'd been mostly type-cast as 'the girl next door'. I thought it was wonderful to be able to portray a character that was a departure from that type. A character that I feel is closer to who I really am as a person, and I could organically depict that strength and independence."

Though the movie would eventually find its audience and become a cult classic, its tone puzzled some at the time. "There were some people in powerful positions who didn't have the same vision as Thom" Catherine recalled. "I don't think they understood what the movie was from Thom's point of view. Thom's original prevailed, thankfully, and in my opinion that's what made it unique, entertaining, and successful."

Casting had its surprises too. Kelli initially had her eye on the role of Reggie. "I originally wanted to read for Reggie, as I was tired of being cast as a kid. She was such a badass character and got to ride a motorcycle had the bike, and beat up a zombie. But Wayne Crawford (the producer) looked at me and said, 'You're Samantha.'"

The decision stuck, and it proved to be the right one. Kelli found a lot to explore in Sam's layered personality. "Sam wasn't just a cheerleader. She wasn't an idiot. She was the Queen of denial, sure, but she was processing things her own way. There's something about that I really liked, it was her way of surviving."

The shoot was often scrappy and inventive, but always memorable. Kelli remembered how simple the special effects could be. "There was this guy just out of frame with a bottle, it was like a ketchup bottle full of fake blood. And he's squeezing it into the tube, and I'm trying to act like I'm terrified while this sticky, cold syrup is going everywhere. It was so low-budget and so hilarious."

Action scenes brought their own kind of joy. "I come from a dance background," Catherine explained. "So when it came to one of my favorite scenes where I fight a zombie in the alley behind the theater, my dance training came in handy. I was strong and flexible. I really got into it, but I knew I was safe and in good hands. The actor who played the zombie was also a professional stunt guy. He was fantastic. I approached the fight like a dance. It was about very specific movement and timing. So much fun. True nirvana for me."

Even the casting of Mary Woronov brought unexpected emotion. "When she came in, I thought, this woman is gonna eat me for breakfast," Kelli admitted. "She plays the scientist. And she is so intimidating… But when we did our scene, she suddenly played it really maternal and kind. And it pulled something out of me, I turned into a child in that moment. I wasn't expecting that."

But nothing stirred emotions like the saga of the cheerleader uniform. Years after production, Kelli tried to recover the original costume she had sold. "My dog had cancer, and I had to pay for the operation. The only thing I had that was worth anything was the cheerleader outfit, that I had kept all those years. I sold it to a collection under this verbal agreement that I could buy it back soon after," she said. "But the guy didn't keep his word. It ended up in an auction where I had to bid on it just to get it back. I was crying so much, it was horrible and embarrassing."

To Kelli, it wasn't just a costume. "It wasn't just Sam's. It was a part of *me*. And fans understood that."

A GoFundMe was soon launched by supporters, who helped her reclaim the outfit. "It's totally safe now, and had been restored. I still owe everybody a photo of me wearing it again. I haven't forgotten. And then after that, it's going under glass where it will stay for all eternity."

As the years passed, the film's legacy only grew, fueled by conventions, re-releases, and emotional stories from fans. Catherine remembered the uncertainty she felt attending her first convention. "I was nervous for my first convention. I thought, 'Who's going to remember this movie?' But people showed up. A lot of people showed up. It blew me away. There have been so many wonderful, inspiring stories from fans. I'll never forget the brother and sister who came to a convention that Kelli and I attended with their little stick figure cartoon book of the entire movie that they had created as young children. They'd watched *Night of the Comet* many, many times on VHS as kids, and loved it so much that they were inspired to create their own animated booklet version. What an incredible compliment."

Kelli's experience was just as moving. "Kids would say, you know, my mom had to work nights, and so she put an Night Of the Comet because you guys were so string, and I felt safe.' And I just cried. I had no idea we had that effect on people."

The movie became a beloved comfort for many, a 'babysitter movie,' as Catherine put it. "People tell us they watched it over and over. They memorized the lines. It became part of their childhood."

But beyond nostalgia, it gave young audiences something they hadn't seen before: heroines who didn't need saving.

"We weren't perfect. We weren't superhuman," Kelli said. "But we weren't waiting to be saved, either."

Catherine added, "Girls could see themselves represented in a movie as the lead protagonists, and they could relate to these characters on many levels. We portrayed strong independent young women but with humanity. Sam and Reg don't depend on 'superpowers' to show their innate power and strength, they are just regular teens from the '80s with their surprising and unique ability to handle some serious weapons because of being trained by their Green Beret father. Guys love the strength and independence of the characters too!"

And it still resonates in 2025. "We've met lots of parents who reflect that they love the message that *Night of the Comet* sends young women, "You don't need to be rescued. You can take care of yourself."

Asked where their characters might be today, the actresses didn't hesitate.

"Sam's still stuck in the '80s," Kelli laughed. "She's driving a patrol car around the ruins, looking for people to save. Still wearing the Flashdance sweater. Probably has a daughter, and DMK will be long gone, probably rebuilding Vegas. Still sassy."

"Reggie is no longer a bored teenager," said Catherine. "She's just a happy little grandma on an organic farm, rocking her grandkids on her knee and thinking, you know, this Mother Earth gig ain't so bad.

While reboot talk comes up often, they're wary of losing the original's essence.

"People want to make it darker," Kelli said. "But *Night of the Comet* wasn't dark. It's a hallmark movie. It had hope. It had love."

"It wasn't cynical," Catherine agreed. "It was about family. That's what made it last."

And for both women, the experience had a lasting personal impact.

"It gave me confidence," Catherine said. "I saw myself differently after that."

"Sam made me brave," Kelli said. "She made me funny. She helped me find strength."

Today, *Night of the Comet* lives on, not just in memes and remasters, but in memories, fan art, and a certain blue and pink cheerleader outfit. More than anything, it lives on in the people who saw themselves in Sam and Reggie.

"We believed in it," Kelli said. "And we still do."

"And we believe in the people who still love it," Catherine added.

The world may have ended on screen, but Sam and Reggie walked forward. And in a way, they've never stopped.

ECHO ON PUBLICATIONS

Official Novelizations
from Echo On Publication

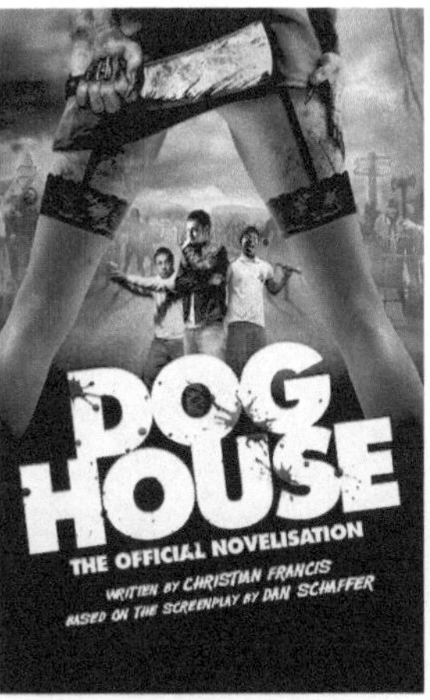

In The Mouth
of Madness

Night of The Comet

Doghouse

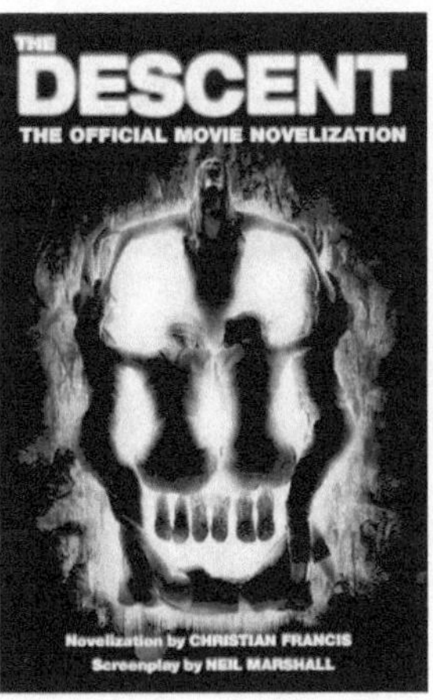

Witchboard

The Gate

The Descent

*In Partnership with
Titan Books*

check echohorror.com for more details

Official Novelizations
from Echo On Publication

**Beneath Perfectiion
(Tremors)**

Session 9

The First Power

Maniac Cop 1,2 & 3
*Avaialble individually or as a
collected hardcover*

**Dee Snider's
Strangeland**

**3615 Code
Santa Claus**

check echohorror.com for more details

Original Novels and Novellas
by Christian Francis

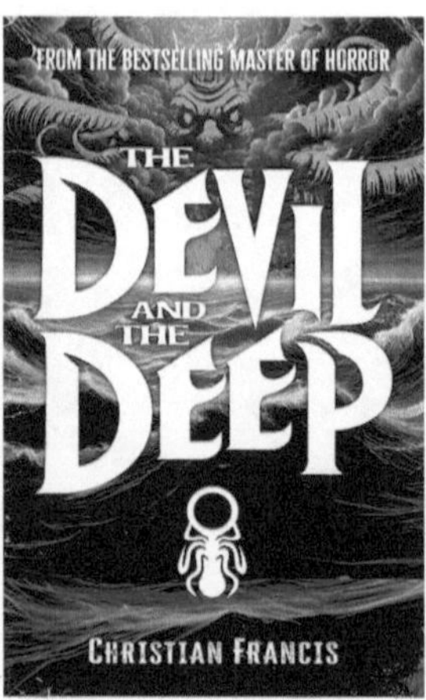

The Dead Woods
YA Horror

**The Devil
and The Deep**
Cosmic Horror

**The Sacrifice of
Anton Stacey**
Horror Novella

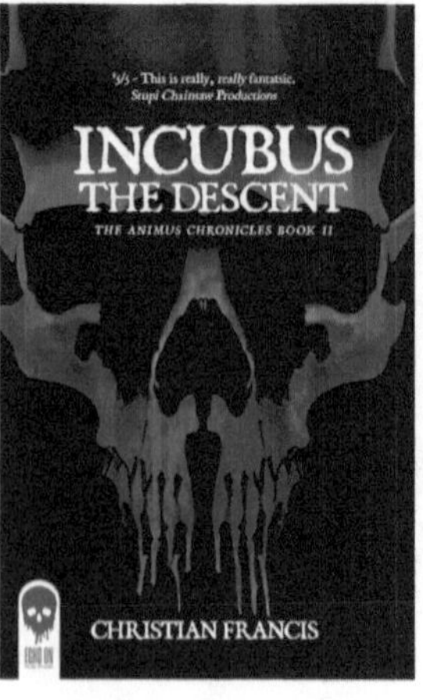

The Animus Chronicles Part 1
Everyday Monsters
Horror/Dark Fantasy

The Animus Chronicles Part 2
Incubus: The Descent
Horror/Dark Fantasy

www.ingramcontent.com/pod-product-compliance
Lightning Source LLC
Chambersburg PA
CBHW060552190726
48283CB00003B/983